BUILD
UNIVERSES

Oliver Salter

M3 Lee and Other Stories

europe books

© 2020 **Europe Books**
europe-books.co.uk

ISBN 979-12-201-0248-3
First edition: November 2020

M3 Lee and Other Stories

M3 LEE

Harris looked down at his hands. They were still shaking. The explosion of air which had ripped through the tank still rang painfully in his ears. They had been hit a few minutes ago, yet still Harris could still feel the shock of the blast reverberating up and down his spine, sending worryingly unnatural reactions to his hands and feet.

He found that his left foot was tapping compulsively against the steel floor. When he saw his boot tapping almost rhythmically in front of the pedals, to the tune of the ringing in his ears it seemed, a strange memory returned to him. He remembered a Fred Astaire picture he had seen with Lucy at the Electric on Portobello Road, before he was called up. It was as if his left foot, making music to the aftershocks of the shell's crushing impact, was trying to mimic Mr Astaire expertly delivering another show-stopping dance number. The memory departed his mind as soon as it had arrived though.

Dixon suddenly clasped his dirty oil streaked hand on Harris' knee. And the tapping stopped. He looked down with surprise at the hand. It had been browned by the punishing sun and was bearing small circular burns from handling searing hot cartridges. He had been pulled back into the moment. Dixon released his knee from his vice-like grasp, and looked around at the rest of the crew. His round sweaty face strained with panic and confusion. "Now what!?"

The Lieutenant had ordered Harris to drive the tank into the paddy field. He had been determined to pursue his quarry; a mortar team which had eluded them all afternoon. As the M3 Lee tore across the field, kicking up soil and dust around it, the shell had hit.

It smashed into the ground directly to the right of them. The blast shredded the Lee's feeble armour. Fragments of the right side of the tank, together with the shell's casing screamed through the hull. How neither McNally or Kozakiewisz had been hit, let alone eviscerated by the shell was beyond Harris' comprehension. He had felt the air part above him as blades of shrapnel showered the inside of the tank. One piece smashing into the left side the hull, missing the crown of Dixon's head by centimetres. It was almost as if divine intervention had saved them. The Lieutenant who had been standing up in the hatch, exposing himself, hadn't been so fortunate though.

A sizeable chunk of jagged armour torn from the hull must have rocketed up into his face. His body had buckled and jolted under the weight of the impact, stood there motionless for a few seconds in the hatch, before slumping down in the turret next to Ennis. The high-pitched girlish shriek torn from Ennis's lungs was loud enough to heard by the rest of the crew below him. Harris whirled around to see Ennis cowering in the corner of the turret away from the Lieutenant, or rather what remained of their commanding officer. Before jerking his head away in shock, he had glimpsed a cavernous fleshy hole where the Lieutenant's youthful unspoilt face with its thin Clark Cable-inspired moustache had previously been.

That was when he had lost control of the hands and feet. As Harris sat back in his uncomfortable metallic seat, Mc-Nally had climbed into the turret, wrapped his strong arms around the Lieutenant's ruined torso and hauled the body out of the tank into the hole ripped into the ground by the shell. He treated it as if it was a mundane task. His face hadn't betrayed any of the disgust or stress he may have felt.

The inside of the hull was completely silent. Only Ennis's strained heavy breathing could be heard above them. Somewhere off in the distance the continuous drone of a C-47 transport plane on a supply run could be heard, before it eventually faded away. Emanating from the jungle surrounding the field they could hear the sporadic snaps of rifle shots, the slow thudding of a Bren gun and the occasional thunderclap of a shell blast.

They stayed at their stations, waiting for a second round to crash into them. Waiting for the Lee to explode, engulfing them in flames. Waiting for the tank to become their own funeral pyre. Waiting to join those charred twisted cadavers they had pulled from the wreckage of broken vehicles before. But it never came.

It was then that the reality of their situation dawned on them. Dixon initiated the debate; what do they do now? The left track had been immobilised; they weren't going anywhere. Harris had always respected the Lieutenant, but the facts were obvious. He had directed them into an open field away from the rest of the squadron, leaving them exposed and isolated. "Into the paddy, old man!" were probably his last words, and those words had been thick with malice and violent intent. The more that one moment repeated itself in Harris' head, the more its implication disturbed him; he had been willing to put his crew at risk to kill a few more Japs.

They had in fact driven away from the area they were ordered to defend. They had no idea where they were. The location of the other Lees was equally unknown. The boom of one of their 75mm guns could intermittently be heard somewhere off in the jungle, but the much hoped for rumble of tank tracks nearby was worryingly absent. Perhaps the young man had just lost his head in the heat of the moment, Harris thought to himself. The idea of him losing his head was now quite ironic.

As the crew checked the tank's equipment, they found that their radio had been shattered when they were hit. Water was low. The uncomfortable jungle humidity and prickly heat meant they were always thirsty. No food. They had eaten the last of the spam and biscuits that morning, and had been fighting the Japs on empty stomachs since. The ammunition was nearly spent. They had been busy that day.

They had been like firemen; driving up and down the perimeter putting out one fire before moving on to the next. Sometimes supporting the West Yorkshires, other times the Punjabis, on occasion the Gurkhas. It seemed that the enemy was materialising out of thin air, bursting from the jungle and trying to break through everywhere.

As the Japs threw themselves at the perimeter, Trooper Dixon on the 30. calibre machine gun had been cutting them down with escalating intensity. A savage smirk curling across his tanned face, seemingly oblivious to the burning hot cartridges cascading on to his boots and trousers. "Conserve your ammunition!" the Lieutenant would sometimes order to no avail.

Lance Corporal of Horse McNally had been operating the 75mm gun with his typical composure and workmanship, perfected from years of working in the steel mills of Sheffield. A place where a careless decision could have meant losing a hand to a stream of molten iron. Now his work was; load, aim, fire, reload. If he needed to, he could steadily continue unaffected without any delay or even a break for water.

McNally had a calming effect on Kozakiewisz, who would reload the formidable gun with considerable speed and efficiency. He had arrived in the Arakan as a frequently nervous and uneasy young man barely into his twenties. Prone to fumbling with the ammunition when under pressure, he would also yell course playground rebukes to Dixon's underhand comments afterwards. Trooper Kozakiewisz had now become a completely different soldier when the Japs surrounded the whole division a few days ago.

Trooper Ennis though, hadn't adjusted to the situation. He felt the pressure of being positioned in the turret with the Lieutenant breathing down his neck beside him. He shifted erratically in his seat during any heated moment; if a shell screamed overhead, contact was reported over the radio or even if a single Jap emerged from the jungle into view. It was extremely obvious to the whole crew. "Dancing again, Ennis?" Dixon snidely chided once with one of his usual sadistic grins. His handling of the 37mm gun wasn't much better. A whole Jap section once sprinted out of the undergrowth to barely concealed cover behind an abandoned staff car. A stupid decision which Ennis couldn't capitalise on. "Fire, Ennis!" the Lieutenant had barked in his increasingly shrill voice. The shell sailed clear over the Japs before landing harmlessly in the trees beyond. Without the need to be ordered, McNally fired his gun and the Japs disappeared in an explosion of earth and pink mist.

Now Ennis's anxiety and fears had reached the end of their rope. He looked around in panic at where the blood, matter and shreds of skin had splattered; the inside of the hatch above his head, the visor of the gun, his seat, his boots. He let out another shriek which filled the inside of the tank when he found part of the Lieutenant's nose under the collar of his tunic. Harris could only make out of fragments of what the terrified young man above him was yelling about. Something about leaving here, getting out, going home, that he didn't want to die. He was crying in a shrill way which reminded Harris of the Japs' animalistic war cries whenever they charged out of the jungle. In Ennis's thick barely comprehensible farmboy Somerset accent it just sounded like nonsensical babble.

The four men below in the hull starred up at him in stunned silence. "Shut the fuck up!" Dixon unhelpfully shouted; his own voice thick with fear. McNally just observed the scene with his usual cold expressionless gaze. Not a single recognisable emotion etched on his face. Kozakiewisz appeared to be completely taken aback by Ennis's rambling. "Ennis, it's okay! Stop! Toby, stop!' It was no use.

Harris crawled up into the turret and grabbed Ennis by the shoulders. Something needed to be done. "Trooper Ennis, I need you to focus!" the order came out louder than expected. "You're our upper gunner!" The wailing and babbling subsided. Ennis looked at him blankly. "The Lieutenant is gone, you're our eyes and ears up here now". The young man wiped the stream of sweat from his forehead with his hand, and nodded. His breathing remained heavy but he was near silent. "Sorry old man, sir". He sat back in his seat, wiped the smear of blood from the 37mm gun's visor and looked through it.

Harris eased himself back into the driver's seat, all three men in the hull looking at him. In a war picture there would have been a big speech about duty to your friends and to your country, but there was no need. Ennis just had to be told what he needed to do.

McNally pulled the Lieutenant's Browning pistol from his belt and wordlessly reached over Kozakiewisz, and handed it to Harris. He must have taken it when he had heaved the body out of the tank. They nodded to each other in acknowledgement. The message was clear; he was now in charge.

Harris was a Sergeant after all. Well, this was a calvary regiment, his actual rank was Corporal of Horse. Seeing as the right track was destroyed and the tank immobilised, there wasn't much use for him as a driver. His purpose was to lead now.

He had only been a leader once before, when he had owned the garage. He had managed all its accounting and affairs, trained most of the staff. He had been immensely proud of that garage and of his team. He had been given the monicker; 'old man' by the crew he now served with. His old team wouldn't dream of giving anything less than the respect he was due.

Some loyal clients his team served included a high-ranking RAF officer, a factory owner and the son of an earl, or something like that. One had called the shop the most efficient and professional garage in London. A complement which made him almost burst with pride. Then war was declared.

The team either volunteered straight away or was called up later, and dispersed all over the world. They disappeared into the vastness of the events taking place in nearly every continent and ocean. One of the most senior mechanics had last been heard from at Dunkirk, but no word had come through since. Harris was particularly wounded to hear that a young man he had trained from the very beginning had been on the HMS Hood. Then one night in '41, a bomb had landed squarely on the shop, erasing it from existence. Harris often pondered what the Luftwaffe's gripe was with a small garage nestled between a barber shop and a pub just off Holloway Road.

He had received his own letter from the War Office not long after, telling him where to report to and when. Lucy had cried all night. "You're too old, what would they want with you?!" It's a question that would never be answered, and he found himself on a transport ship to India a few months later.

"I think we should vote". They had exhaustingly spoken through each option for their next course of action. Harris would interject every time he felt that they were taking too long to reach a decision. Time was not with them.

Dixon and Kozakiewisz had done much of the debating. Despite all their petty bickering and exchanging of childish insults over the last few months, Harris was surprised to see that they agreed on the same idea; leave the tank and run back to the squadron.

Where was the squadron though? Harris thought. They had as much chance of running into a Jap patrol. Or reaching the perimeter and getting shredded by their own machine guns. The second shell hadn't hit for a reason; nobody knew there were there.

Ennis had offered the occasional thought or agreement,

but hadn't contributed much during the debate. He appeared to still be in the process of recovering from shock as the colour gradually returned to his face.

McNally had remained silent the entire time, not giving much evidence that any of the crews' arguments had registered. Not even the occasional nod or shake of the head. When he had thrown the Lieutenant's body out of the tank, a considerable amount of blood had streamed on to his tunic. It had now dried in the prickly heat, caking one side of his battledress yet somehow he didn't seem to care. Harris sometimes wondered if McNally was even functional as a human being whenever he wasn't fighting.

Harris had suggested that they vote, which Dixon gave a frustrated sigh to answer with. Kozakiewisz tried to explain in a more civil tone. "With all due respect old man, we can't stay here" He ventured to lean over and lightly grasp Harris by the shoulder, not keeping with strict military etiquette when addressing an NCO. "We could be behind the Japs' lines for all we know". Harris gave a stony glance at Kozakiewisz's hand, still resting on his shoulder. The loader met his gaze and abruptly withdrew to his seat, looking slightly surprised.

"We vote" Harris reiterated. This time we made sure that he sounded sterner, and followed it up with a searching at the whole crew around him.

"I vote to stay here". Harris then turned to the machine gun servant to his left.

"Dixon?"

The desire to leave was immediately repeated. Harris turned to his right.

"Kozakiewisz?"

The loaded just nodded forcefully in agreement with Dixon "McNally?"

He didn't know what to expect from the hull gunner. But the reply came; "We stay"

Kozakiewisz anxiously inhaled. Dixon shot McNally a surprised glare, but then broke off eye contact when an intense stare was returned.

"That leaves you Ennis" All four of the men in the hull looked around at the upper gunner in the turret. Only his boots and trousers were visible. There was silence for a few moments, and Harris briefly thought Ennis hadn't even been listening.

"I think we should stay"

The sun was starting to retreat behind the hills to the east, the last vestiges of its rays reaching across the jungle towards the tank. As he peered out of the driver's hatch, Harris shielded his eyes from the glare it produced. The field in front of him was now illuminated in an orange glow. It gave Harris a strange, now unfamiliar sensation; peace. Both sides evidently felt the same, as the sounds of fighting gradually faded away. Men exhausted from the trials and exertions of another demanding day settled down to a restless night in their uncomfortable slit trenches under the darkness of the jungle canopy.

Now there was a different adversary assaulting the crews' senses and endurance; the smell. The odour of hundreds of bodies scattered across the jungle, decaying and bloating under the unforgiving sun of the Arakan, rose up from the earth and blanketed the battlefield. Out of the blue, Ennis abruptly observed; "English, Indians, Japs. They all smell the same when they're dead" It was the first thing he had said in hours, and drew an irritable glance from Kozakiewisz and a poisonous look from Dixon.

Inside the tank was no refuge. None of the crew had washed in over a week, making the air oppressive. The lack of any breeze entering the tank made it hard for everyone to stay at their positions without shifting awkwardly, as they tried to find the best way to escape the smell which invaded their nostrils and slipped down to the back of their throats.

Outside the tank, the buzzing of flies swarming around the Lieutenant's body in the shell crater had become an incessant humming. It constantly was in the background as they tried to rest, observed the field in front of them for movement, made a count of the ammunition they had left, made mundane small talk about trivial things to keep distracted. It was inescapable.

Night eventually settled over the Arakan, and the crew tried to get some sleep. McNally volunteered for sentry duty. He didn't need the sleep.

Harris leaned back against the hard steel of his seat and closed his eyes. He wondered what Lucy was doing at this time, thousands of miles away in Islington. It was probably the early afternoon, so she might be out doing her daily food shop at the local green grocers. He pictured her examining her shopping list through her reading glasses, which she would possessively do every other minute, making sure that she had everything. He wondered if she had managed to procure those much sought after but strictly rationed strawberries she had mentioned in her last letter. She had waited in line for close to an hour only to find that they had sold out.

He thought about what she might do afterwards. He heard that there was a new picture with Cary Grant out, who she was slightly partial to. She might go see that. Oh yes, he just remembered that she included in the letter that her youngest sister's fiancé had just returned home from service with the RAF on Malta. Apparently, he had been flying Spitfires. If he had been younger and had less of a belly, Harris often thought that he could have made a... then the night erupted.

To the left of their position and behind them, the jungle was now alive with gunfire and shell bursts. Two searing white Very lights hung in the air above the tank illuminating the field in a ghostly pale glare. Orange streams of tracer rounds flew in all directions.

McNally immediately manned the 75mm gun, ready for the Japs. Kozakiewisz had been jolted awake when the fighting started, banging his head on the underside of the gun. He loudly let out a slew of foul curse words in both English and Yiddish as he crawled over to man his position next to McNally. Dixon aggressively cocked the machine gun, and searched through its sights for the expected attack. "Where are the fucking yellow bastards?! Where are they?!" Ennis had snapped awake with a startled gasp and thrown himself forward on to the 37mm gun. His finger was precariously curled around the trigger.

Harris searched through his hatch. There was no sign of any movement in front of them, the fighting seemed to be confined to the trees to their left. He anxiously eyed Dixon next to him, who looked ready to spray the field with what was left of their 30. calibre ammunition. Ennis was almost pinned to the visor of the gun, his index finger was obsessively mimicking the pulling action needed to fire. He too looked prepared to send shells flying across the field with his usual inaccurate fire. Firing discipline needed to be maintained.

"Do not fire!" Harris ordered over the din of the firing. "Do not give away our position" The crew do not fire. They stayed rooted to their positions, anticipating a wave of Jap infantry to emerge out of the darkness, charging through the white glaring light towards them.

In the trees, they could hear men yelling and screaming. It was impossible to discern if the cries were in English, Japanese or any of the languages the Indian Army troops spoke. Every gun in the Arakan seemed to be firing around the field. All they could do though was to stay at their positions, and weather the storm.

Morning came, and the attack on the tank hadn't come. The bitter odour of sulphate and cordite hung heavily in the air. It had been a helluva fight, as one of those American airmen they had played cards with back in Calcutta would have said. That now felt like a lifetime ago.

Smoke drifted through the trees, sweeping past the Lee. Peering through his hatch, Harris thought that the sheets of white smoke crossing the field smoke looked like the banners of a phantom army. It looked like something from one of those short cartoons that played before the main feature.

With the break of day, the heat also returned. Sweat dripped off Harris' forehead onto his face, stinging his eyes. He could feel large wet patches formed around his armpits and lower back, making his undershirt stick to his torso. Water was alarmingly low. They had been carefully rationing it, but it seemed to be constantly dwindling. Harris' lips were now painfully cracked and dry, and his voice only capable of making a rasping whisper.

The whole crew though was now in the depths of an uncomfortable hunger. They hadn't eaten since early the previous morning, and that breakfast had consisted of meagre portions of unappetising bully beef and blocks of cheese which were a chore to consume. Kozakiewisz hungrily reminisced about the journey from Calcutta, when the American personnel manning their LST had treated them to huge steaks and bottles of Coca-Cola. He described in uncanny detail how two of the Yanks had looked at each other in shock when he had told them that one of those steaks was equivalent to his family's weekly meat ration back home. Dixon predictably told him to shut up.

"I think the Lieutenant had some chocolate in his haversack" Ennis suddenly remembered. They had been trying to figure out how to procure food from somewhere. Everyone in the hull turned around to see Ennis' surprisingly eager face looking down at them from the turret. He may have been on to something. The Lieutenant never took off his haversack, not even in the confines of the tank. "In the event should an undesirable situation arise" he had declared. It had practically remained glued to his back the entire time they had been in the Arakan.

"But wouldn't it be outside then?" Kozakiewisz apprehensively asked. He turned to McNally next to him, who nodded in confirmation. "Yes...but it was in his haversack, the flies wouldn't have got to it" Ennis cheerfully answered. Every one looked at each other puzzled. Harris tried to summon some breath from his dry throat to explain the dangers of what he was proposing, but Dixon interjected anyway. "You're missing the point! What if a sniper sees you?" A brief pause "Or worse a fucking artillery spotter?! Then we're all fucked!" Ennis looked nervous, but for a brief moment. He tried to force an uncharacteristic optimism again.

Was he trying to make some sort of contribution? Was he ashamed of what happened yesterday, and this was him making amends? Harris thought about these questions as he thoughtfully looked up at the young man. There seemed to be flinches of desperation pushing through on Ennis' smiling face, which clearly some façade. "You don't need to prove anything" Harris croaked.

Finally, the real Ennis started to come out. His face creased with nerves, he looked nearly as scared as had yesterday. "Look, we don't have any food. We don't know when the rest of the squadron will come get us" He looked around at everyone, as if desperately appealing to them. "I'll be quick, I'll grab the chocolate and come back. Trust me!"

Harris looked out of his hatch again. At present the smoke was fairly thick as it glided across the field. It could conceal someone's movement as long as they didn't linger. He turned back round to Ennis and pulled the Lieutenant's pistol out of his belt. He gingerly handed the sidearm to the upper gunner. "In case you run into trouble" A slight smile flickered back to life on Ennis' face "But be quick" Harris had never had children, but in that one moment he felt like a father giving strict but thoughtful commands. Ennis nodded, before reaching up and opening the hatch.

They listened in silence as Ennis closed the hatch behind him and clambered down the side of the Lee. There was a sound of earth being shifted as he slid down the side of the shell cater. The flies gathered around the Lieutenant's body buzzed with more intensity as they dispersed with the arrival of an unexpected intruder.

Dixon looked at Harris with a mixture of annoyance and scepticism. "He's more likely to blow his own foot off with that pistol than find us any food" Harris ignored him. The chocolate, if it was even still in that haversack, would probably have turned into brown sludge in the heat. Yet he felt that Ennis needed this. He wanted to show everyone that he hasn't a burden, that he could do his part and help them all.

Suddenly, there was a shocked yelp from outside. This was followed by a sharp crack of the pistol being discharged. The crew all snapped alert. There was a second pistol crack, then a third, then several more. There was a metallic clunk on the side of the tank as someone jumped on to it, several more as the person desperately scaled the side of the tank.

The hatch flew upon and Ennis almost dived inside. He looked like he had been thrown back into the state of shock he had spent much of the day before. He was barely in control of his breathing, which was erratic and sounded like it was being torn from his body. The pistol shook in his sweaty hand, smoke still whispering from its barrel.

Dixon and Kozakiewisz looked at him in a state of bewilderment and fear, while McNally studied him with a scrutinizing look. "A Jap! Outside!" Ennis eventually blurted out. Several heads looked at each other, then to Ennis again, then through the sights of their guns to confirm what he said.

Harris felt as if a great ball of lead had just dropped to the bottom of his stomach. He swallowed nervously. "Are you sure it wasn't one of the Gurkhas?" That was a stupid question, none of those stocky brown-skinned Gurkhas looked anything like the Japs they'd seen. "No! It was a fucking Jap! I saw him!" Ennis almost exploded

"I didn't see him" Dixon abruptly interjected, sounding very defensive "McNally, did you see anything?" The gunner shook his head. "Are you saying I'm a liar?!" Ennis yelled with a ferocity which took Dixon a back. Harris stared at the pistol in Ennis' hand cautiously. In that moment, he felt there was not much from stopping the young man from emptying the last of the magazine into Dixon. That image instantaneously flashed in front of his eyes, and he felt another rush of fear course through his body.

"Listen!" Kozakiewisz threw up his hand, imploring them to stop. They stopped and listened. Voices. Outside, in a strange language. They couldn't tell how many.

Dixon slid his arms into position on the machine gun. McNally fixed himself to the gun, his hand grasping the trigger. Ennis tightened his grip around the pistol, he looked ready to fight. Kozakiewisz leaned across and mouthed some words to Harris; "What do we do?" The voices came closer. They were clearer now.

Harris didn't know what to do. This was something they couldn't possibly have been covered in the training they give to new NCOs. Did the voices belong to a section of Indian troops investigating a seemingly abandoned tank? What if they weren't on their side? Even if they were, the crew wouldn't want to take any chances. He simply didn't know what to do.

There was a clunking sound from the back of the Lee. Someone was climbing on the tank. A savage snarl contorted on Ennis' face, baring his teeth like an aggressive dog whose territory was being encroached on. He looked up at the hatch, his arm slowly rising into a position to fire directly into anyone who tried to come in.

More voices. All from either the back or the right of the Lee. There wasn't a thing Dixon or McNally could do, their guns being of limited maneuverability. Kozakiewisz reached for an entrenching tool under Ennis' seat.

Someone's muffled voice sounded directly above the turret. Ennis rose to his feet, the pistol's barrel now almost touching the underside of the hatch. Harris raised his hand, pleading with the young man "Ennis, don't-" the hatch opened.

35 YEARS

6 August 1880

I arrive in london one month ago.

Everyone says it is the most amazing city in the world. But I think it is so dirty and smelly and every day have rain. I am living with my uncle in a place called limehouse. I hate it. So many people here are drunk and live in streets. Many people get sick and die here. But there are other people from Guangzhou. I am happy at that.

I do not want to be here but mama says I need to. We do not have any money after baba die. She say I need to go to London and work for my uncle. She says I need to help her and my sisters.

I am nineteen year old. But I need to help my family. they took our house in Guangzhou. Mama and my sisters now live with her sister. I want mama to be happy.

Uncle tell me I need to make my English better. He give me this diary to write in. I go to a very good school in Guangzhou and I learn English but I do not like it. but I need to speak it very well now. I think write in this diary can help me.

11 November 1882

Today they beat me again. They are sailors and they hate all Chinese. They call me chink and filthy yellow.

So many people don't like me. They look at me very angry when I walk on the street. Children throw things at me sometimes.

I don't have any money. My uncle pays me very little. When I do have money, I smoke the poppy in my uncle's house. Or I have the drink. I cannot spend money on the women though. They don't want to have a chink.

I cannot send any money to mama. Sometimes she send me a letter wanting to know where is the money. Sometimes I do not read the letters I throw them away.

I hate here. I want to leave. I am angry and sad every day. Sometimes I am so sad I want to die. I cannot go home though. Mama will be angry if I come back with no money.

Maybe I will leave London but go to America. I can get money there and then go back to Guangzhou. But I think they will hate me and call me chink there too.

I have no happiness. I only have this diary.

22 June 1887

I am very excited. My business partners sent me a telegram. They said that the girls will be in London soon.

I began to steal from people and cheat them when I was very desperate, but it gave me more money than I expected. Mama is very happy with the money I send her. But I want her to be proud of me now.

I left my uncle's house. I told him what I think of him. I told him just owning an opium den and lending money would never get him success or respect. He will always just be a chink. He said I was ungrateful. He said I was a bad man who lies and cheats and never wanted to see me again. But I don't care what a stupid old man says.

Baba was also a stupid old man. He spent so much and gambled with everything including my inheritance. So when he died we had nothing. The debt collectors and lawyers took everything. I will not be like them. I will think about the future now. I am a thief and a criminal but I will not be poor.

I decided to change when I was beaten by the Irish man who was angry with my uncle. He beat me so hard one of my eyes almost fell out. I still cannot see from that eye. So I took a big knife from the butcher and went to find him. I found him as he was drunk and cut his face and his belly. I cut him many times.

After that day, I felt I was a strong man. I made many friends who work with me now. I found my business partners from Hong Kong. They travel to the foreign-owned ports like Shanghai and find the girls.

The girls have no homes or their families are poor. They

tell them about how wonderful London is and how they can find rich husbands there and live very happy lives. They then send them to London and they will work for me.

All men like to feel that they are in control of other people. Every man feels this way. Rich or poor. Chinese or English. A man who says he does not is lying. I will give men what they want with these girls. People who think they are good will say I am a bad man. But every man who became rich does not care about what is good.

18 May 1895

Tonight I put on my best suit and went to the theatre; a new production of Hamlet has just opened at the Royal. Afterwards I went for a stroll around Covent Garden and found the most expensive restaurant possible.

I was alone but I certainly didn't feel so. Wherever I went, numerous pairs of eyes would follow me. The sight of an exceedingly well dressed with an air of authority and dignity indulging himself in luxurious surroundings is hardly a rare sight to any of these stuck up, spoilt, unworked snobs who frequent the theatre district. But if that man is a Chinaman, and one with a pale white blind left eye at that, then that truly is another matter.

Their intrigued stares, bewildered gazes or contemptuous looks are all a drug to me now, and a far more addictive drug than any dirty little opium den could ever provide. Because it all reminds me of how far I have come.

Business has been good. What else can I say? Of course, I lied to and exploited all of the girls, but they did their job and made me rich. If they want to leave, they always can. But very few do. Some make their money and return to China. Some decide to move on and leave for the United States or places as distant as New South Wales or the Cape Colony, and continue to apply their trade there. Some find husbands; a sailor or a dock worker or another immigrant for instance and settle down here in London, raise families and try to forget their past. But there are always more girls to replace them.

I now have maybe over a hundred girls working for me across this city. Wherever it be working the filthy dockside taverns in Stepney, or attending those debauched rich man parties in Kensington; I have girls for every occasion and every taste.

I know what people think of me, the ones that know what I do. But I am too busy thinking about my next goal and how I achieve it to care what they think. Especially those who work for me. They keep their mouths shut and do what they're told. I have found that I have a talent for making people fear me now.

Speaking of goals, I have accomplished what I originally set out to do all those years ago. I regretfully write that since I have last written in this diary, Mama passed away. But because of what I provided, I assured that she died in a more than comfortable *siheyuan* in Guangzhou with about dozen servants tending to her. It certainly was a better life than Baba could give her.

One of my sisters used the money I sent to attract the interest of a successful Dutch architect. They got married about two years ago I hear and live well in the International Settlement in Shanghai. My other sister decided to emigrate to Penang a while ago, and I haven't heard anything from her since.

I am pleased to write that I have even more good news. I am to be married.

I am thirty-four years old now and find myself in need of a wife, as any successful man's life is incomplete without one. I am already successful, but understandably very few men in London would let their daughters marry a half-blind Chinaman with such dubious business interests. Fortunately, I am acquainted with Mister Horrwitz.

A German Jew who has made his name through being an especially gifted tailor, he found that very few worthy men wished to marry his eldest daughter; Jennifer on account of her being a Jew. I find that a special type of hatred is reserved for Jews in London. The Irish and Italians are just about tolerated, the *lascars* and blacks are treated with open disdain, but the Jews are hated with a real passion by most, rich or poor.

While he was taking my measurements one afternoon, we got to talking on the matter and I suggested rather spontaneously that I could marry her. He appeared to be slightly taken-aback at first but then warmed to the idea, and arranged for me to come to dinner and meet her.

Jennifer Horrwitz is a lovely young woman. Sweet, intelligent and good natured. She didn't seem uneasy about my blind eye, or at least did a very good job of not showing it. As we met more, we found that we shared many common interests. We would speak at great length about literature and theatre, as many of the writers which helped me acquire this standard of English proficiency are usually the ones that inspired her as well. She also would ask me many questions about China, and about my upbringing.

I was confused by this at first. She was the first English person to show any genuine interest in where I was from. But I came to realise through her fascination that my home-country is a special place, that has been unfortunate enough to fall on very hard times. For a few days, I found myself actually longing to see my home again after almost fifteen years away. I amended this brief period of weakness though by proposing to Jennifer. She accepted.

As I write this diary entry late into the evening, the candle on my desk dimly illuminating the words on the page, I cannot help but feel an almost immeasurable self-gratification. Tomorrow I will be looking into moving out from my lodgings here in Limehouse and view some more spacious dwellings in the West End. I will then report my findings to Jennifer. I would not be planning that day if I hadn't taken the path I did years ago.

A Chinese man cannot even gain wealth or anything resembling respect in his own country, let alone in a foreign country. The Chinese man of today will find that only a Manchu with the right connections can succeed in China, and in any other country he will just be seen as a lowly chink capable of very little. The course I took allowed me to escape this fate.

You may judge me and call me immoral, a man with no decency or sympathy for others. Your words will simply fall on deaf ears though. I am proud of the man I am now, and I certainly won't make any fucking apologies.

24 December 1903

The Christmas decorations are finally all up, so I can sit in the living room and write this without any concern of being disturbed. There is a small mound of seasonal greeting cards on the coffee table that remain unopened, possibly from Jennifer's relatives or my business partners. I shall ask our maid; Magda to attend to those once she has read little Suzie her bedtime story. That would usually be Jennifer's job but she is understandably rather exhausted under the weight of her pregnancy. "It will be easier the second time", she usually says with an air of insincere optimism about her.

Jennifer surprised me the other day when she suggested that next February we should celebrate the Spring Festival. Her reasoning was that by that time the baby would have been born, and it is important now to teach our children about their Chinese heritage. It was strange for two reasons. Firstly, she hasn't shown any interest in giving Suzie a Jewish upbringing. Secondly, I will of course always be Chinese but it feels now that trying to reconnect to my homecountry is beyond me. I have been through too much now to simply turn back.

I went on a business trip to visit my company's supplier in Hong Kong last year, but that was the closest I have ever been to Guangzhou since I left. I could have easily taken a ship up the Pearl River to where I grew up. Visited family I had not seen in over two decades, or reacquainted myself with places that meant much to be when I was a boy. But I decided against it.

I lied to myself at first; that the mounting unrest and

anti-foreign sentiment in China worried me. As a wealthy businessman with obvious connections to the West, I would make myself a target if I returned. In reality it was because an insurmountable barrier, my very own Great Wall erected itself in my mind. China is a poor, backwards country enslaved to the will of a hopelessly corrupt Imperial family who are now very much in servitude themselves to foreign powers.

If China were a person, it would be someone I would refuse to associate myself with. Because truthfully, it was the person I once was. I reiterate what I previously wrote. I won't turn back.

I am to a certain extent still in touch with my country though. It was at Jennifer's insistence due to her interest in all things Chinese that I became involved in the porcelain trade, or 'China' as it's more simply called here.

I have been very fortunate this year especially, and our porcelain has been shipped around the world. The British in particular seem to have a strange fascination with this product and Jennifer was right to encourage me to take advantage of that. From the gardens of Surrey to the hill stations of Bengal, English ladies and gentlemen have had their afternoon tea served to them with my porcelain.

It does not just mean that our children will have a considerable inheritance to look forward to when they grow up, but they will know that their family name is a respected one that really means something to many people.

That previous business I was involved in; I left it. I didn't dissolve it, sell it or pass it on to someone else. One day shortly after Suzie was born, I simply left the office I kept above a warehouse in Greenwich and never came back. Nobody dared contact me after, as by this point quite a few people were too scared of me to seek me out. I am now paying for those days.

Jennifer made it clear to me when we got married that she did not want to know about my business and would never ask, as long as I remained a good husband. I only told her about the girls or anything to do with the business after I started having those nightmares. At night, a particular incident kept revisiting me for some time.

It was the winter of '96, a sailor who had just returned from overseas went beserk and beat one of the girls to within an inch of her life. I don't know the provocation was, if there was any, but when I came to the inn on the Isle of Dogs where it had happened, I saw that he had beaten her until her nose was displaced pulp sitting awkwardly on her cut bleeding face. Her eyes were swollen shut, her teeth scattered on the floor around her and she appeared very close to death.

The other girls understandably were out for blood, and demanded that I find the sailor and bring him to them for retribution. One of them was very serious about castrating him and turning him into a eunich for the rest of his life. I firmly told them that no such action would be taken, and that this needed to be kept quiet. I don't know whether it was the shame of my insensitive decision or the image of that bloodied dying girl seared into my memories, but it was an evening that has always stayed with me. There had been several other incidents like that that have also resurfaced unexpectedly as if to taunt me. The one with the butcher's knife and that drunken Irishman most notably.

Perhaps I should keep this entry briefer. I shall try to write more additions to this diary, make it a duty of mine from now on. I found it earlier today as I was retrieving the Christmas decorations from the attic. It was in a pile of old ledgers and business journals.

I read through some of the pages and marvelled at the naivety, anger and arrogance written on them. I will keep this diary very close to me from now on. I think it is now imperative to remind myself to be a good man.

Anyway, I believe I shall now find Magda, tell her that she can go home and bid her a Merry Christmas. I shall attend to the greeting cards myself.

10 October 1915

Suzie has locked her herself in her room for close to two days now in her grief. She has refused all her meals, and we are all very worried about her.

Jennifer pretends everything is alright, she reads a book down in the living room but very obviously is putting on a façade. I've told her several times that she is ruled by her emotions too much to convincingly adopt that English stiff upper-lip. Magda has stationed herself outside Suzie's bedroom, anxiously waiting for any signs of movement from inside. In his confusion, little Alexander will sometimes walk up to the door and gingerly ask, "Do you want to play a game, Suzie?". He will then trudge back downstairs in disappointment after hearing no reply.

At first her reaction confused me as well. She had made it very clear that she had no intention of marrying young Freddy Miller from the start, much to mine and Jennifer's relief. She is only eighteen years of age, and has far too much intelligence and talent to get married so early.

"I don't wish to live my life like one of Emperor Hongwu's concubines', she smugly declared one evening at dinner, hoping I would appreciate the reference to Chinese history. She doesn't yet realise though that that kind of arrogance for a young lady and rejection of the status quo will make her a social pariah in English high-society.

Although Freddy's intentions were good, he was clearly acting under the influence of his father; a very unsympathetic man who owns a law firm and clearly just wanted him to marry a girl with a sizeable inheritance and a good name. She had rebuffed him several times. Distraught, he went off to war against his father's wishes, and two days ago we received word that he had been killed in Flanders.

It becomes clear to me as I write this that she isn't grieving because she loved Freddy, she most certainly didn't, but because she feels an immeasurable guilt. She is aware that he died having been rejected and humiliated by the only women who he felt serious about enough to propose to. She is probably feeling right now that she is someone who ruins others. Yes, I think she has inherited those beliefs from me.

I have tried to give Suzie and Alexander the best possible life, even if it has meant distancing them from me sometimes. I was the one that insisted that they take Jennifer's family name; Horritz. Taking a Jewish name was still better than going through life with a Chinese name and be reminded every day how different they are from everyone else. My company is called; 'Horritz Porcelain' so they did not have to be seen as a yellow-skinned slant-eyed chink like me.

But everything worse about me, the bouts of self-loathing and extreme guilt especially seems to be something I have not been able to protect her from. In addition to being probably the smartest person I've ever met, she is one of the best and kindest as well. There is however a gene in my family which makes us either give in to our vices or fall into despair easily.

Baba certainly had it. He lost everything through his selfishness and greed, and when he realised that, drank himself to death before leaving us all in squalor. I on the other hand collapsed into self-pity so catastrophic I wanted to die, and then told myself afterwards that it was okay to use others for horrible purposes to climb the ladder of mobility. I will pay for it in the future.

I don't subscribe to the simple-minded Christian belief of Heaven and Hell, but I am convinced that I will answer for my crimes one way or another. What I need to do now is save Suzie from this fate as well.

I think I should stop writing now. I will go upstairs and speak with her. I need to tell her to step back from this path that she may take. What exactly I will tell her, I am not sure. But I think I need to tell her more about my experiences, my life. Jennifer has explicitly forbidden me from ever sharing such details with our children, but I feel if you want someone to be good person, you should tell them what it is to be bad person.

SONJA

Blood poured from the girl's nose, down her lips and front on to her dress. Yet it did not seem like she was in pain in the slightest. She continued to stare up at Viktor with those innocent, blue eyes, her face an expressionless mask. Viktor reckoned she was in shock, and what had happened had not hit her yet. But it was almost as if she had anticipated this. The weeks of hiding in cellars, cowering from shells and rockets tearing the streets and buildings above her to pieces, and praying that the Russians did not find her, could only be concluded like this.

Viktor himself hadn't had more than an hour's sleep these past few days. His eyelids tried to shut, and his stubble irritated his face. He stunk of sweat, cordite and his own urine. Just a few hours ago though, news had broken that the last German troops in Berlin had capitulated. Now he was stinking drunk, a bottle of vodka in hand, hoping to forget the last three years. Three years of marching, hunger, freezing cold nights, comrades being killed in front of him. Now he was going to release the collective anger and grief welled up in the pit of his stomach, gathered through all his miserable ordeals into this girl, this German girl.

Viktor's comrades pulled the girl out of a cellar, along with two teenage boys of about fifteen both wearing *Volkss-*

turm uniforms which hung off of them and a tall middle aged, spectacled man in an SS greatcoat. He towered over his captors, who spat abhorrent insults at him, batted his cap off of his head and tore at his SS insignia. To their astonishment he replied in flawless Russian; 'Fuck your mother! Sub-human dogs!'

As two of Viktor's comrades started to tussle over the girl who screamed for help, the others preceded to viciously beat the boys, who cried and pleaded and the SS man who endured their blows and kicks with great dignity. Even as blood streamed from a gash in his forehead, and several of his ribs snapped under their boots, he seemed to accept his beating and humiliation as a formality that needed to be accepted. Suddenly Vova; a 19-year old Ukrainian, pulled a pistol from his belt and fired it point blank into one of the boy's skulls. Blood and brain matter splattered the girl and the man holding her, who screamed loud enough for him to let her go. At this point, Viktor grabbed her as Vova fired another three shots into the second boy's head, reducing it to pulp spread out on the pavement. Men jumped back to avoid being shot in the feet. The SS man did not even flinch at this sight, and even looked at Vova somewhat carelessly as the young man withdrew a bayonet from his bloodied boot, and grabbed his captive by the hair and pulled his head backwards exposing his throat. Viktor turned with the girl just as a hot spray of arterial blood showered the back of his tunic. He ran with her in his arms to a nearby air raid shelter.

Now there she was. Sitting at the wall in this dark shelter which smelt of shit and mould, holding her torn dress together, blankly staring up at Viktor through her mattered blood-stained hair. How was he going to do this? When he had seen other Russian soldiers rape a German girl, sometimes they had resisted, screaming and clawing at the men's faces and eyes or biting their ears like a wild animal. They were then put in check by a few hefty blows to the face. Others simply accepted their impending torment, lying still as the man on top of her thrusted down into her. One or two did not even show much pain, and instead whispered a prayer under their breath. But this should not be too hard. The girl was pretty, though Viktor was very drunk so there was a risk of not being able to perform as well he would have liked, and embarrass himself. The girl was very pretty in fact, with her large blue eyes, perfect skin and curled brown hair. She reminded him of Sonja...yes, Sonja.

Viktor had barely thought about her for three years now. She was a memory locked away at the back of his mind. Now everything about her flooded forward. Her smile mainly, and the feel of her hand in his. In the village on the banks of the Don where Viktor was born and grew up, he was always seen as too small and awkward to gain any sort of respect. His brothers and the other boys in the village relentlessly teased him at his inability to perform the most menial of physical tasks out in the fields. He was weak, and his physical weakness made him mentally weak as well. He became an embarrassment to his father. He was skinny, skinny enough for his ribcage to be visible when he was bare chested, his face seemed to stretch over his skull, and his arms were like twigs. He had no place in an unforgiving landscape and way of life. But inexplicably, Sonja liked him.

Sonja was by far one of, if not the prettiest girl in the village. Most of the other girls were jealous of her, and spiteful behind her back. She was aware of this, but paid no notice. The biggest, strongest and therefore most confident boys would frequently try to impress her, or sometimes go as far as propositioning her. Once again, she paid no notice. Then one day when Viktor was feeding the chickens, to his great surprise she came over and said hello. She smiled her charming smile which put him at ease, and even laughed when he ventured to tell a very bad joke. They continued to meet for long conversations and walks over the next few weeks. Her presence gave him a confidence which made him feel as strong as the other boys, who felt an intense jealously seeing a weakling like Viktor with Sonja. In fact when they were seen together in the village or in the fields by her admirers, Sonja would hold his hand close to her or go as far as kissing him on the lips. They both took great satisfaction in seeing rage visibly bubbling up inside them at this sight. Sometimes Viktor himself couldn't understand why she was with him. When he would ask her this, she would simply laugh.

After a few months, Viktor gathered the courage to ask Sonja to marry him. She said yes. The wedding was an affair which involved the whole village; there was plenty of drinking, dancing, and everyone congratulated Viktor. His father finally looked at him with love in his eyes. A tough, remorseless man who had lost a hand during the Brusilov offensive, only to return to a life of hard labour and poverty had now finally accepted Viktor as a son.

Viktor remembers it was one bright afternoon in March, no April 1942 when that all changed. He and Sonja had been married for nearly a year now, and she was four months pregnant. He was returning from another disappointing foraging trip when he saw trucks belonging to an *Einsatzgruppen* unit spotted a few days ago moving through the area. They were driving into the village. He immediately dived to the ground in one of the fields, and watched them dismount from their vehicles and start ushering people from their homes. They dragged the old and infirm, and started to punch, stamp or hit with the stocks of their rifles the ones moving too slowly. They searched each house, looking for those who were hiding, sometimes emerging with a struggling infant in their arms. They moved everyone to the centre of the village, out of Viktor's view. When the machine-gun fire and screams started, Viktor leapt to his feet and tore across the fields, desperately working every understrength muscle in his feeble body. He only looked behind when he reached the dense forest nearby, and saw a tower of smoke staining the horizon directly over where his village would have been.

Viktor joined a partisan unit camped in the dark depths of the forest. For the next year Viktor found himself partaking in a merciless guerrilla campaign. The shock of losing Sonja and his family had not quite registered, so killing the Germans was only to be motivated by survival if need be rather than hate. When the partisans captured an SS officer and proceeded to torture him, Viktor fled to his shelter, refusing to watch. He clasped his hands over his ears with a strength he didn't think he was capable of, shutting out the German's bellows as they castrated him.

When the Red Army recaptured much of the Smolensk region just over a year later, Viktor was conscripted into their expendable masses and the next two years were one long hard march to Germany. As the struggle to stay alive became an everyday reality, the memory of Sonja and the unborn child she was carrying slipped to the back of his mind like a cloud passing on the horizon. Even with all the women in the Red Army, finding another woman never occurred to Viktor. They were just other soldiers to him. The single thought dominating Viktor's existence was making it through each engagement, rather than the home and family he was going to have afterwards.

Now he was in Berlin. The Soviet Union's victory was complete; fascism had been ground into dust. Viktor could hear above him men celebrating in their various languages and dialects, getting drunk, firing their rifles and machine-guns in the air. Soon many of them will go home to the lives they had before, and readjust to being a civilian again. Viktor however didn't have a home; his village had been burned to the ground, he would have nowhere to go. He also didn't have a family anymore; his parents and siblings had all been murdered along with everybody else he knew. Sonja was dead.

As this truth hit him like a bullet, Viktor dropped the bottle of vodka in his hand, its contents spilling out across the filthy floor. He put his hands on his shaved head and let out an animalistic cry torn up from the depths of his body. The young woman who had changed his life, and was to give him a child truly was gone. The life he was going to share with her had been taken from him. The girl on the floor looked up at him more intensely than before, as if even her shattered mind-set had comprehended that this wasn't usual. Viktor let out another agonised sob; 'Sonja!' As the name escaped from him, his knees buckled under the weight of his grief and fell to the floor. He sat in the dirt and his spilled vodka. Through his tears he looked at the girl in front of him, who returned the stare. Like him, she had lost everything. But Viktor had only just realised it.

THE CHAPEL

Dominique keeled over on his horse, as the pain from his two broken ribs intensified. He desperately sucked in a big gulp of the cold mountain air, as it now felt like a huge fist was mercilessly squeezing on his insides. His horse slowed to a stop beneath him on the wooded path. 'What's the hold up, savage?!' McCarthy's voice boomed up the path, momentarily sweeping away the silence of the mountain.

Dominique turned around to glare at McCarthy, who was sitting there sternly on his horse with his gang all perfectly assembled behind him. All nine of them staring impatiently at their guide up front. Gritting his teeth, tearing up what must be his last ounces of determination from the depths of his stomach, Dominique pushed on further up the mountain. His captors following suit.

As soon as McCarthy and his gang, a thrown together bunch of labourers, farmers and former soldiers, were finished beating Dominique the previous night, descending on him out of the darkness while he slept, the anger at his present circumstances seeped into his mind and quickly overwhelmed him. Anger that he had come to California in the first place, anger that he had chosen to prospect in a gorge in the middle of nowhere filled with men that wanted to kill him, and anger especially that he had told Terrence about the chapel.

As they force marched him up the mountain, he tried to let acceptance of his predicament push away the violent rage festering away inside him but it was hopeless. He kept telling himself that he had made many mistakes and would learn from them, but it was pointless. He wasn't going to live long enough to see out the day. When he had led them to the chapel, McCarthy's boys were going to kill him, leave his body up on the mountain for coyotes and vultures to gorge on, and his mother back in Ohio would never know what had happened to him. Upon this realisation, it was despair instead that took over him.

Dominique thought that maybe he had told Terrence about the chapel because he had felt sorry for him, he was perhaps the only man in the gorge that was lower down in the hierarchy than him. He had arrived in the gorge wearing an expensive fur coat brought from back east, and gave everything around him a quizzical, slightly anxious look. Dominique knew that he would not survive long without help, he was someone that others would prey on.

A spectacled quiet bank clerk from Hartford, Connecticut with a thin pale face and twigs for arms, Dominique decided to stick with him and eventually they prospected on the river together. He helped Terrence adjust to the alien and harsh conditions of the wilderness that his new companion was struggling with every day, and in turn he helped Dominique feel a little less alone in a place where anyone with his skin was immediately not welcome. Although they never found any gold, they became good friends and the only ones each other could trust. He had actually told

Terrence about his discovery of the chapel over a bottle of whiskey.

Now Terrence was riding with McCarthy's boys at the back of the pack, looking deeply ashamed of himself. He refused to look at his friend, and instead would hang his head so he was looking down at the path under him. Dominique strangely did not blame him though. He was desperate, as was everyone else in the gorge.

An icy breeze swept down the mountain. Dominique felt another sharp stab of pain as his body tensed against his broken ribs, and the cold stung the huge swelling on the side of his face. One of them had kicked his face several times, leaving his left eye so swollen it was forced shut.

McCarthy was now riding alongside him, giving him an intense unrelenting stare down at him from under his bushy red beard. Dominique did his best to avoid meeting his stare. 'This the way?'. Dominique nodded quickly. 'You sure, boy?'. Another anxious nod.

From this close up, Dominique could very clearly see the long unpleasant scar which crept down his forehead, along his cheek before disappearing under his unkempt mass of facial hair. It was mostly likely from a drunken brawl in a saloon or cathouse back east, but the campfire story went that it was sustained while fighting Indians on the Plains. If it were true, it might explain why McCarthy hated 'the dirty savages' with an unbridled intensity.

Dominique could handle the general stores that had NO DOGS NO INDIANS signs in the window or the occasional retort of 'stupid savage' or 'filthy redskin' here and there, but it wasn't until he arrived in the gorge that he felt he might be killed because of his appearance. He bore little resemblance to his father; a trapper from Quebec, but instead had inherited the dark skin and pitch-black hair of his mother, who was of the Shawnee Nation.

These men had given up everything to do with their former lives back east, risked life and limb travelling across the Plains, to arrive in a gorge where they thought they would make their fortunes but only found rock, snow and failure. They were angry. And having banded with McCarthy, as the strongest figure in the gorge they now shared his hatred for anything that looked slightly like an Indian.

Upon hearing Terrence's story about a chapel up in the mountains, where the Indian had found the fortune they came to California for, they knew that this was most likely their last chance.

A steep precipice greeted them at the end of the path. The valley in its entirety lay before them down below. The snow topped redwoods forming a seamless green and white blanket covering the mountains and stretching off towards the horizon. 'Now what?' McCarthy growled at Dominique, his beard dotted with snowflakes. The captive gestured with his head up the mountain, where the path continued to climb through thick undergrowth and densely packed trees. McCarthy's cold expressionless eyes narrowed to form a suspicious look. 'I aint lying' Dominique assured him weakly.

Dominique had already fallen off his horse once, his body simply too battered, too broken to have the will to continue up the mountain. He had landed squarely on his shattered ribs, which ejected an animalistic wailing sound from him which echoed across the valley.

From there onwards, McCarthy had placed him under the charge of Guillermo, who had reluctantly agreed. McCarthy had then ridden up ahead to scout the path with Hennessey; a farmboy from Georgia and a cruel, bad natured soul who also had a gullible mind that was easily bended. 'Wanna see f'myself if the savage aint bullshitting us' he spat in Dominique's direction. Before they departed, Dominique overheard Hennessey try to discreetly ask his companion; 'When can't we jus' kill the damn savage?'. It was at that point when something awakened in Dominique.

Guillermo must have been a decent man before he arrived in the gorge. He was honest, uncomplicated and being Mexican himself was able to empathise with Dominique's position. In fact, the small dejected looking figure now in Guillermo's charge, hunched painfully over his horse had even considered him one of his friends.

The pair continued up the path in silence as McCarthy and Hennessey gradually disappeared from view. The rest of the group trailed behind as usual. The fire that had now been light in Dominique's belly after hearing Hennessey's confirmation of his death sentence, was telling him one simple thing; to survive and to try anything that would allow him to do so.

'What makes you think McCarthy is gonna share whatever's up there, Guillermo?'. The words effortlessly slid out of his mouth. Suddenly he was now confidently sitting upright on his horse. Guillermo abruptly turned to stare down at him, widening his brown eyes in surprise and looking slightly confused at how quickly their captive's demeanour had changed. 'What did you say?'.

Dominique had more words to follow up. 'Do you really think he gives a shit about any of you?'. He gestured his head back at the group behind, all looking more pained as the weather grew more bitterly cold as they ascended the mountain. Guillermo bitterly looked away, as if to say that he would not listen to the lies of a deceitful half-breed. 'You betta shut your mouth' he threatened without any real conviction. Dominique could see that his words had seeped into his thoughts, and were now digging deeper into him as he thought more about them.

Guillermo was a reasonable and practical man. Far more than most of the other mindless sheep who had flocked to McCarthy. And best of all for Dominique, who was someone that others would listen to. He therefore ventured to appeal to Guillermo's common sense and hidden feelings of anger and bitterness more. 'He said he was in the Mexican War right? What makes you think he likes your people any more than mine?'. While McCarthy's war stories were most likely more of his self-invented tall tales meant to gain a flock, Guillermo actually had fought in the war but for Mexico. It was because of the war, that his mother and father had lost their farm and livelihood in Texas, meaning that he had to pick through the rock for segments of gold that was never there to support them.

By the time Dominique had finished recounting to Guillermo all the times McCarthy had shown his selfish, hateful and violent nature since they had both in the gorge, he could see that he was starting to cause a conflict within him. The Mexican simply looked on ahead silently with a sad, mournful expression. He had never told his prisoner to shut up or threatened him with another beating, but just listened. He knew he was right.

When Guillermo gave everyone permission to rest for a short while, a flash of relief exploded in Dominique. He doubled over his horse and swallowed more frantic mouth-

51

fuls of air. The higher they climbed, the colder the weather became, and the more the pain felt like it was twisting and tightening over his stomach and lungs. Every time the freezing wind swept over the exposed, painfully stretched skin covering the now enormous swelling on his face, it felt like a drill was pushing into his skull.

They had stopped because poor old Remy could not continue anymore. The oldest of the group, he had picked up a reputation as a very tough man who had spent his life in extreme poverty in the Louisiana bayou but had somehow kept a good natured and unwaveringly positive outlook and was much liked by everyone. His anecdotes about his time as a drummer boy at the Battle of New Orleans quickly entered camp folklore, and were often retold with new details added in every time.

A week previously Remy had fallen clumsily off his horse and scrapped a good deal of skin off his knee on a sharp rock. He had laughed it off at the time and had insisted he was fine, but now the untreated wound had turned gangrene.

Dominique had been ordered to stay on his horse, but as he uncomfortably strained around to see what the commotion was behind him, he could see the short and stocky figure of Remy helplessly slumped against a tree. He had lost the use of his bad leg and could not carry on.

Guillermo and the others gathered around him, debating what could be done next for Remy while at the same time desperately giving the old man assurances that it was going to be alright. They all knew though that there was little though they could do for him near the summit of a mountain, as no one had the expertise or necessary equipment to treat such a bad wound in the wilderness. This unwanted and hideous truth hung over them, and everyone refused to acknowledge it.

Terrence however was anxiously pacing up and down along the path away from the group, stretching his long legs into big strides, his hands held behind his back and looking down at the frozen ground mournfully. He looked like he was attempting to come to terms with the inevitable.

Remy himself also was fully aware of the reality of his circumstances. In between his long-agonized groans, he pleaded with the group in his thick Cajun drawl to leave him behind, that he was of no use any more and that they should go to the chapel and get rich for themselves.

As everyone seemed to collapse into a state of indecision and despair, the sound of horse feet beating against the dirt path drew rapidly closer. The bearlike figure of McCarthy perched atop his horse emerged into view, Hennessey trailing not far behind.

For the first time since Dominique had had the misfortune of knowing McCarthy, a big toothy grin was cracked across his ugly scared face. He dismounted heavily, splashing the mud beneath him up on to his fur coat. 'The redskin aint lying!' he declared, but even his deep booming voice failed to break the oppressive silence. Everyone just awkwardly looked at McCarthy and then to each other, Guillermo was only able to manage a hopeful nod in their leader's direction.

McCarthy was taken aback by the absence of cheer created by his news, and his usual confrontational posture meant to intimidate those around him quickly returned. He saw that most of the group was gathered by the tree where Remy lay, and angrily stormed over to see for himself.

The men trying to help Remy parted as McCarthy arrived to examine what the problem delaying his personal quest for wealth and fortune was. Remy looked up at him with a meek expression, as McCarthy bore down on him. As he stood over the crippled man, he swiftly looked over the wound, and without any gesture or change of expression to indicate his decision, made up his mind in a few seconds.

'Leave him'. He strode back to his horse, while most of the group gave each other shocked and helpless glances. 'He aint useful no more, leave him'. Everyone remained rooted to where they stood, too stunned by the idea of leaving their friend to die. Only Guillermo looked unsurprised, slightly regretful as he realised that this is something he should have expected when he banded with McCarthy.

McCarthy turned around, his face tightening with anger at seeing their reluctance. Dominique could a rising tide of fury building in him, as his body stiffened upright to its fullest, most intimidating stature. He then rounded on Guillermo, staring down at him with his pair of piercing blue eyes which seemed to be silently burning with white blanket of rage.

Guillermo simply raised his head slightly to meet McCarthy's stare. He wasn't afraid of him, unlike everybody else, but he maintained a forlorn and reluctant demeanour. Hennessey watched with great amusement on his horse, eagerly anticipating the confrontation to escalate, a big grin revealing his unsightly brown teeth.

'Is it jus' gonna be me and Hennessey?'. McCarthy's words were uncharacteristically delivered in a silent but intense way. Hennessey's grin broadened into an ugly smirk.

They had carried on. All except McCarthy and Hennessey who continued to lead from the front, looked deeply ashamed and disgusted with themselves. Studying their glum depressed expressions, Dominique could tell that Guillermo felt emasculated and that his self-pride had taken a huge beating. Terrence looked queasy, as if the image of a pack of coyotes emerging from the forest and feasting on the dying Remy had been constantly replaying in his head.

Dominique however felt that the fire in him was growing. As shameful as it was to think, he was extremely pleased that Remy had been left to his inevitable death. This band of misfits, failures and renegades had only been united through desperation, and possibly a few of McCarthy's lies. But now the deep divide that was barely hidden before, was plainly on view for all to see. And the way Dominique saw it, if the chances of them resorting to their more primal nature and turning on each other increased, then so would his prospects of escape and survival.

Suddenly up ahead, small traces of civilization started to grow out of the undergrowth by the path. Gravestones; a handful of them became visible as they stuck out of the soil. Several of them had been nearly destroyed by the years of erosion at the hands of the harsh weather. The others had been gradually reclaimed by the forest, as an assortment of vegetation now covered them in a constrictive embrace which completely obscured the names of those buried below. Most of the group looked at the gravestones with great curiosity as they passed by, wondering how anyone could build anything meant to replicate an ordered community this high in the mountains.

This was now a familiar sight to Dominique however. When he first discovered the chapel, these gravestones were like a mirage appearing unexpectedly out of thin air in this vast, forgotten stretch of wilderness. They had possibly been the first evidence of a society he had seen since he had arrived in the gorge a few months before, and they had beckoned him to continue up the mountain towards his discovery.

And sure enough after a short ride further up the path, the chapel loomed out of the forest in front of them.

When he had first found the chapel, Dominique could only assume that it had been built by Spanish missionaries here to educate the local savages into becoming good Christians. How long ago? Having grown up in the forests of Ohio, he was not the right man to judge. In his experience any way as a man of the Shawnee, the building of churches on the land that rightfully belonged to the people who lived there, was usually a declaration of war on their heritage and culture.

As the remaining eight men dismounted, they looked up at the chapel in amazement at how the construction of a mainly stone building in the Southern European style was possible in such an isolated and foreboding place. There was not much left of it though, the roof has been largely stripped away under decades of storms, the windows had mainly been smashed leaving only a few shards of glass standing in the frame of…

A pair of hands grabbed his coat roughly and pulled him off his horse on to the hard, cold ground. He landed heavily on his hipbone, and the pain shook his whole body and the impact reverberated up and down his spinal column, rattling his already broken ribs. The air was knocked completely out of him, and he helplessly rolled in the dirt in shock trying to adjust his body to the sudden explosion of agony.

Hennessey stood over him, looking deeply satisfied with himself, a sadistic grin spread across his pockmarked face. His narrow slits for eyes bearing down into the Indian flopping around like a fish on the ground. Behind him stood McCarthy, watching impatiently as Dominique regained his composure. He lay on his back and looked up at McCarthy with visible anger rising to the surface of his face. 'You gonna show us where it is, boy?'

Dominique limped across the dusty, shattered interior of the chapel. Broken pieces of wood from the benches were strewn across the floor, and the floor creaked under his hobbled walking. Rain water dripped down from the ruined timbers above them.

McCarthy followed closely behind Dominique, who was now reduced to a painful limp. The rest of the group curiously followed a few feet behind McCarthy with Guillermo clearly attempting to overtake Hennessey.

With much effort, Dominique eventually reached the small altar at the head of the chapel, which had somehow survived the years of abandonment and exposure to the mountain's climate. He awkwardly positioned himself behind the altar, supporting himself on it. McCarthy stood just in front of the altar and watched Dominique, the tension in his face betraying that he felt that this surely had to be the end result of months of disappointment and discomfort. The rest of the group stood motionless in the centre of the chapel watching the pair of them expectedly, except for Guillermo who pushed his way to the front.

Dominique eased himself down and reached into the sizeable hole in the wood at the foot of the altar. He briefly felt around inside before finding what he was looking for. He pulled out a medium-sized dusty old wooden chest.

McCarthy lurched forward to study the chest, his eyes looking at it hungrily. There was a murmur of anticipation amongst the group, and Guillermo stepped forward for a closer look. McCarthy aggressively gestured to Dominique to open it, who obliged.

McCarthy studied the contents of the chest with a mixture of greed, amazement and hope. All three emotions sparking to life in his eyes. He then snapped it shut before Guillermo arrived to see for himself. The two then stared at each other for a while, silent threats being made between them. Dominique backed away slightly. He could see anger bubbling away under Guillermo's usually composed exterior, which McCarthy had recognised but wordlessly communicated through a sharp glare that he should back off.

He then took the chest and thrust it into Dominique's arms. 'Go to my horse, put it-', but Guillermo had already withdrawn an old Mexican Army-issue pistol out of his belt.

Dominique slowly emerged from his hiding place. The chest clutched close to his body. He ducked out of sight behind the altar when it had all started. Now all he could hear inside the chapel were a few agonized groans from one badly injured man who sounded like he was on his way out himself. He was first greeted by the sight of McCarthy and Guillermo locked in a deathly embrace on the floor, the pure rage and animalistic desperation to kill the other still etched into their faces.

Guillermo had admittedly squandered his advantage of surprise by allowing his uncontrollable anger get the better of him. His lack of composure and sound judgement had travelled down his arm to his shooting hand, and he had only managed to blow McCarthy's left ear off and a hole in his shoulder when he had his back turned. It evidently hadn't been enough.

Dominique had witnessed McCarthy pull out his formidable hunting knife and lunge at his attacker in a rage, screaming a savage war cry, before he had dived for cover. He had then heard two more pistol blasts, and the two of them tussling on the floor, their cries of fury and pain as they had brutally maimed one another. Cries which eventually lowered to whimpers and gasps before stopping all together.

Now Dominique could see that McCarthy had driven his hunting knife through Guillermo's stomach, still wedged in there, standing perfectly upright in the Mexican's body. He then looked up to survey the scene of carnage and despair that assaulted his senses.

It seemed that when McCarthy and Guillermo had launched themselves into a fight to the death, a realisation that it was in fact every man for himself had been unlocked in each member of McCarthy's band. The months of suffering at the hands of the merciless weather, cruel abuse from their fellow prospectors, and the agony of failure had created a swollen river in them all. A river which had now burst its banks. Their loose bonds between them had disintegrated in an instant and they had turned on each other, a mass brawl erupting there in the chapel. They had attacked, maimed and killed one another with knives, tools, fists, teeth, anything that would inflict pain.

Dominique picked his way through the bodies heaped on the floor of the chapel. The unnatural contortions of their bodies, which had been broken under the pressure of the savagery of their attackers created images which seared their way into Dominique's mind. He knew that he would take these sights to the grave. Some had had their faces battered into shapeless ruins or their limbs broken or their eyes gouged.

Only one of them looked alive, and that was only evident from his long-distressed moans escaping from a mouth choked by his shattered teeth. His name was Phillips, a short balding Army deserter. His eyes bulged up at the grey skies visible through the cavernous hole in the roof, but Dominique did not stop to help him in his final moments. He was too bitter at their betrayal, how they had attacked him in his tent, and humiliated him. Stripping him of his dignity by using him as some kind of sniffer dog. Making him feel like a damn savage. As far as Dominique saw it, Phillips deserved no comfort.

But then he saw Terrence's body, slumped against one of the benches. His head arched back, and his face somehow expressionless as it looked up at the sky. He was surprised that no feelings of anger or bitterness reared their ugly head inside him, only ones of sadness and regret. Regret that a good man such as Terrence had come out to a land seemingly only populated by the wicked and greedy in the first place. Regret that he never had the opportunity to tell this man that lay before him that he understood his actions, and that he was forgiven.

It looked like his friend had not even tried to defend himself or fight back, as his held no weapon in his lifeless hands, one of which was still clasped over the gaping stab wounds to his belly. There oddly seemed to be a kind of serenity about the way he had left this world, and this slightly comforted Dominique. If there was a Heaven, Terrence was surely there now.

As he limped out of the chapel, Dominique was greeted by an icy wind whistling through the trees and enveloping him, as if a frost giant had suddenly grabbed hold of his body. The shock of it almost made him drop the chest in his hands, but as his body tightened to resist the cold, he clung to his prize with greater strength and determination.

Several of his horses had been scared off when the slaughter inside the chapel erupted into motion, but his own had remained and he hobbled towards it. He then was met with the pleasing sight of a badly injured Hennessey crawling through the mud.

It looked like he had been stabbed about a dozen times in the legs, sides, chest and most ironic, in the back. Dominique let out a self-satisfied chuckle to himself on that thought. He edged forward eagerly to examine this pathetic, feeble figure crawling like an animal towards his horse, letting out shrill agonising cries every time he pulled himself forward. He then looked around to see Dominique, who grimaced at his badly cut, bleeding face.

'Do…Dom…D', he stretched an arm out. He wanted help. At this, the anger flowed to Dominique's head like a stream of molten lead. 'Fuck you, Hennessey!'. He kicked mud at his face. The injured man gasped as some flew into his open mouth. It wasn't enough though. Nowhere near enough.

He lurched forward to where Hennessey lay and threw his body weight behind a powerful kick, which collided with his former tormentor's nose. There was a satisfying crunch and a shriek. Pain shot up his leg, but he still landed another kick in the form of a savage stomp to Hennessey's head. Then a third one. And another. And another.

Dominique's whole body felt like it was in pain. He still forced himself upright on his horse as he made his down the mountain to avoid further discomfort, but the sheer relief and delight was overflowing in him. Every time the horse's hind legs moved, the contents of the chest strapped down behind him clinked together. It was a wonderful sound.

A huge smile was carved into his swollen face. It actually hurt to smile, but he didn't care. His very loose, sketchy plan to turn them on each other had worked. He had survived, and better he had the chest. He laughed to himself at how it had all been so unlikely, and how it all had worked out for him. And it was a big laugh drawn from his belly, which echoed through the trees and down the path.

First, he needed to find a doctor to fix his ribs. Of course. Then he would sell what was in the chest. He knew what was in there, and it would fetch…a lot, that was all he knew. Then what? Would he stay in California? Just move down south where the climate was more agreeable. Would he go back east? Ohio and the Shawnee sounded like a welcome sight he thought he would never see again.

Buy a farm? Buy the best clothes? So whitefolk would not see him any more as a dirty Indian. Invest it somewhere? Oh, what the hell…his plan first and foremost was to live. He was going to live, and that was the greatest fortune of all.

COMING HOME

The crack of a pistol pierced the air behind the soldier. This was followed by a brief shrill animalistic cry. He whirled around at the top of the gangway to see the horse collapse heavily on to the hard concrete of the dockside.

The soldier watched with surprise, the pavement was almost awash with the blood pouring from the huge hole in the horse's head. He knew that the Army were now selling its horses to the locals, who were starving. He didn't really think much of it until he had seen the life of one of these animals unapologetically snuffed out. So many of these horses had seen the very worst of it. The mud, the shelling, the gas. He had seen them hauling guns through the quagmires of Ypres beyond the point of any living thing's physical limits. And then that was it. They were not going home like everyone else.

'Out the fucking way!' barked the big Corporal behind him. The soldier hurried to the top of the gangway and on to the ferry. He was able to catch a final glimpse of the dock worker who had been holding the horse recoil in disgust at the blood and brain matter that had splattered his hands and trousers. He looked furiously at the Belgian soldier who had shot the creature, who just returned an amused grin.

As the ferry pulled away from the dock and started its

journey across the Channel, the excitement amongst the men built. It had been almost four years, and now the realization that they had made it had collectively sunk in. The relief turned into sheer unbridled joy, which swept infectiously around the ferry. The soldier though just found a quiet lonely corner. He laid his pack and rifle down against the wall, and sat down. He felt he needed to process what he had just seen. His surprise had turned into a deep inescapable sadness.

An animal or not, that horse had probably fought as well as any of the men here. It had most likely endured uncountable terrors, and lost plenty of friends too. It should have been on a ferry going home too, but that was it. It had fulfilled a purpose, and now was only good for its meat. Were all the boys who had gone to the front and not coming home either the same? When they had been thrown at the machine guns and barbed wire it now seemed like they were disposable meat that had fulfilled a purpose as well.

It had been roughly four years now since the soldier had last seen his home near the Thames in Wapping. And the first thing that hit him was the smell. Of course, he had been repeatedly exposed to the sickening stench of rotting, dismembered and half buried corpses littering No Man's Land after a Big Push, but this felt strangely new. A sea breeze swept up the estuary, and blew the various vile smells into a big invisible fog. Raw sewage, rotting vegetables left in the street, black smoke from dozens of chimneys and furnaces, animal shit. It all formed into a toxic cloud, and passed through the street for a few moments.

As the soldier stopped in the street, he felt the soles of his boots slip slightly against the slimy cobble stones. He held his breath as the smell overwhelmed him. It was a surreal thing. He had grown up here. He had spent all of his life here, until he enlisted. He should be used to the sometimes-overpowering haze emanating from the river. But now it was unfamiliar.

As he continued his way through the small filthy streets to his parents' home, he could feel the watery mud in between the cobble stones splash on up to his formally immaculate boots and trousers. He hoisted the sack of possessions he was holding up on to his shoulder to avoid the dirt. He grimaced to himself, as he felt the tail of his greatcoat drag against the surface of the street behind him.

A gang of barefooted children, dirty faced and stinking, wearing torn ragged clothes ran past the soldier, screaming in delight as they chased each other through a puddle streaming from an open drain. The soldier leapt back to prevent his uniform being spoilt further, just in time as a middle-aged woman emptied a chamber pot from a window above. The contents of the pot splashed on to the street directly in front of him. He looked up with an irritated glare at the woman, who just returned a stony look before disappearing back inside.

The soldier continued on his way to his old home. An emaciated mangy greyhound tentatively fed on thrown out scraps from a fishmonger's. A drunken old sailor stumbled out of a dockside tavern, and violently threw up on the floor, soaking his battered old shoes. The same children from before pulled chunks out of pile of horse dung and started throwing it at each other.

The same kitchen which harboured many early memories for the soldier, felt very small and looked extremely dull. Even wearing his greatcoat, it felt bitterly cold. Mother had fed him a simple supper of bread and some meat, and sat down at the opposite end of the table. Her eyes scrutinised him the whole evening. Father sat next him, only a few inches away, beaming and kept on holding his shoulder. Father remarked proudly on how smart and handsome he looked in his uniform, how big and strong the Army had made him. Mother just strategically pointed out that he was eating the last of their butter ration for the week.

He told them all about his war, only reflecting on the good memories of course. How Notre Dame cathedral looked on the inside, watching Charlie Chaplin pictures in a tent full of American troops, a captured Prussian Guards officer shaking his hand and congratulating him on a 'good war', witnessing the Bengali lancers charge into battle. Father's great big smile spread with each anecdote, while Mother's face seemed to tighten with envy and disapproval. At the end of the evening when it was time for bed, she simply told him that tomorrow morning he should hang up his uniform and go out and look for a job.

The local butcher hired the soldier on the spot, a few minutes after he had walked into the shop asking for work. 'I need a boy working in the backroom' he remarked with a satisfied smile which light up his round moustached face. He promptly handed him an apron, and lead him to the backroom. His job would be cutting the animal carcasses into smaller sections ready to be packed. Simple but hard work the butcher told him, he had then laughed to himself and told the soldier that it should not be too hard though for someone that butchered Huns all day long.

All day, every day the soldier would cut, slice, chop and hack sheep or pig bodies into chunks. The thick congealed blood would splatter against his apron, coat his hands, run down from the chopping board on to his shoes. One time, a particularly bloated corpse spurted a mixture of fluids up into his face as soon as soon as his knife made contact with its skin. When the shop closed, he would try to urgently scrub the dried sticky blood off of his hands, making determined but futile attempts to dispose of the blood lodged under his fingernails. The familiar metallic odour would cling to his clothes, and follow him home and everywhere else he went.

Upon arriving back home, Mother insisted that he be in bed no later than eight. As she was back to being his old commanding officer again, the soldier reluctantly agreed. One night he overheard the pair of them bickering. Father insisted on taking him out and buying him his first pint, but Mother kept repeating that he was still a boy that had to be kept on the right path now. A boy? Is that what he still was? Just because she hadn't been there with him the last four years it meant that he hadn't changed to her. He didn't feel like a boy anymore. At least he hadn't at Devil's Wood or any of the other battles.

One day in the backroom as the soldier was prying a lamb's front leg away from its shoulder, the image of Private Willis falling against him outside of Cambrai flashed across his eyes in an instant. His right arm torn off up to the shoulder by flying shrapnel. Although the memory came and departed in a split second, it had felt incredibly real. He could almost feel Willis bleeding profusely all over his tunic again. He stood there motionless, the blade still in his hand, as he looked intensely at the chasm he had made in the lamb's shoulder. Once the image of Private Willis crawling feebly towards his severed arm had left the soldier's mind, he continued with his work.

The next day as he was pulling a pig's head away from its torso, the memory of Sergeant Grey's skull exploding under the impact of a marksman's bullet flashed in front of him. This time he had to sit down and take a few deep breaths of the rancid stinking air of the backroom.

This became more and more frequent, and one day when the soldier finished work, he did not go straight home as Mother always instructed him to do so, so he would be in time for supper. He instead went to a local tavern which he knew Father and the other dockers sometimes went, but he had the intention of forgetting it all. He felt that what everyone expected of him was, that he would just return to how life was before he enlisted, and carry on like the last four years did not mean anything. If anything, all that time was a distraction away from continuing the normal routine of working, finding a girl, getting married and so on.

That evening seemed to pass like a blur. The soldier had of course been drunk before, but out of happiness at times when he was celebrating with the men of his platoon the brotherhood they shared. Now he was trying to push the anger brewing inside him further down, as he was resigned to the reality that simply forgetting was impossible. Those memories defined who he was as a person now.

With each drink though, he started to vent his previously hidden fury to the bar man, to the strangers sitting by him, to anyone within ear shot of him that could potentially listen. The balding portly Russian Jew barman raised his eyebrows in surprise at hearing the fresh faced slight young man in front of him endlessly complain about his present circumstances. Of course, every night there seemed to be a new soul teetering on the brink attempting to drown their sorrows in his tavern, questioning why and where things had gone for them, but this one was much younger than all the others.

The soldier woke with a pounding headache on the floor of the empty tavern the next morning. The barman had been kind enough to throw a blanket over him. It took a few moments for him to figure out where he was, as his eyes adjusted to the dull sunlight pouring in through the window. Suddenly the dual terror of never making it home last night and that he had work now grabbed his insides. He leapt up in a blind panic and ran out on to the street.

Upon his arrival at the shop, the butcher had aggressively grabbed him by the collar and hauled him into the backroom. He glared down at the soldier, his chubby face red with fury. He launched into an explosive tirade about how the soldier was lazy, easily distracted, slow, inept, finishing each sentence by adding the word; 'boy'. He continuously referred to him as 'boy', and each time he said it, it felt like a hammer blow to the soldier's pride, his self-confidence, his place in this world as a man, a man who had endured more hardship than most others. His hands started to curl into fists, and his jaw clenched. All the while the butcher was endlessly yelling at him, insulting him, belittling him, humiliating him, the animal carcasses continued to sway on their hooks behind him.

Finally, the soldier felt something explode inside him like a huge hidden mine, and he throw out a fist towards the butcher's face. The blow was a lot more powerful than the soldier had expected, as his boss' head jerked back and blood fountained out of his nose. The soldier watched in horror as the butcher collapsed against the carving table, and slumped to the floor in a daze. His eyes rolled in their sockets, and the blood was now streaming down on to his apron.

Looking down at the unconscious butcher in complete shock, the soldier quickly uncurled his fists. He had no idea what to do now. Did he call for help? No, he would be thrown in jail. Think of how ashamed Mother and Father would be. Instead he turned around, and simply left the shop.

The soldier had never been to this part of the Docklands before. The buildings and streets had stopped looking familiar a little while ago in fact. He had aimlessly wandered down the river for a long time, and now as the evening had drawn in, he was hopelessly lost. He didn't dare even think about what was happening back at the butchers' shop, or even worse what his parents were doing right now.

The streets were pitch black now. All the lights were out except for the orange glow from a tavern at the end of the street. The light crept across the pavement towards him, seemingly reaching out for him. The soldier stood there motionless as a bitterly cold breeze whistled past. He could hear drunken laughter from behind the tavern's windows, as he considered his options. He still vaguely remembered what had happened last night, and certainly did not want a repeat of its consequences. But he was far from home now, and the night was getting a lot colder. He told himself that this time he would control himself, and then strode towards the tavern.

The old sailor continued to throw more insults into the soldier's face. They were getting obscener, more vulgar the longer he refused to rise to them. The soldier didn't really know what had started the altercation. Had he accidently spilt some of the sailor's drink perhaps? But he now found himself outside in the street again, with this old man asking him for a fight, who was using every foul word his irrational, alcohol riddled mind could think of to provoke the soldier. The soldier however did not budge, he just stood there still watching this old man.

He studied the bloodshot eyes, the sunken haggard face contorted with pointless rage, the weak skeletal figure only just covered by a tattered old coat. He realized that if he continued the way he had been today, he could very well end up in this alley soon asking a stranger for a fight as well. The thought terrified him.

Without saying a word, he turned around and walked back towards the street. Maybe he should find a way home now. The old man's furious taunts followed him as he left the alleyway, but he didn't care. Enough fighting for one day. Tomorrow he would find a way to right his…something slimy and wet hit the back of his head.

Was it rotting food? Was it excrement from some animal? Either way, he could feel it sliding down the back of his neck and under his coat. He could hear the old man cackle in self-satisfied delight behind him. The laughter echoed off the walls of the alleyway, and rang in the soldier's ears. He could feel his whole body stiffen with rage. Before he could even think about it, he had turned around and charged back down the alleyway. In an instant he had knocked the old man to the ground with a heavy thud, and was on top of him.

The soldier rained blows down on his tormentor's face. It felt like he had lost all control of his arms as he constantly withdrew one fist to land another punch with the other. A burning white blanket of unrestrained anger had descended over him.

He could hear the old man make muffled pleading sounds, as his nose cracked and teeth shattered under the repeated blows. The soldier could feel the crunch of breaking bones beneath his fists, and warm blood splatter up on to the front of his coat. An agonizing pain started to shoot up and down his right arm, he must have broken something in his hand. He further aggravated the pain with each punch, and gradually slowed down.

The instant he stopped, he realised what had happened. The old man's face was now a mask of red, as blood streamed from huge gashes torn into his cheeks and forehead by the soldier's attack, which had exposed some of his cheekbone. One eye was swollen shut, while another stared upwards blankly. Only a few jagged teeth remained, the rest were either scattered on the floor around them or had been forced down his throat. The soldier could see his throat rise up and down slowly, but could not hear any signs of life. With an almost unhuman gurgle, the old man suddenly coughed up a fresh spout of blood.

Cold sweat dripped down the soldier's face. He could feel himself turn pale as he looked down at what was left of the old man's face, and felt sick to the bottom of his stomach. The thought of what he had done made him take a few desperate gasps of air. Stunned, he tried to get up but found that his legs gave way beneath him and he collapsed against the wall. He had killed in battle before, but in most of those circumstances it had been either him or the other man. However, he had never attacked another person before that couldn't fight back.

He sat hopelessly against the wall, and watched the old man's chest eventually stop rising up and down. He let out an agonized sob as the implications of what he had done struck him. When he returned home, he had been full of hope about the person he might become. He just never anticipated that it would be this type of person.

ACROSS THE MOOR

An icy Artic wind swept across the moor, carrying the smell of smoke with it. The Winter cold stung the farmer's face and hands, and penetrated him to his bones. But it was that all too familiar smell of smoke invading his nostrils that made a surge of dread rise up in him. The Conqueror's soldiers were continuing to expand their passage of death and destruction across the land.

Yet despite that feeling of fear welling up in him, and a voice whispering in his head telling him to turn back, the farmer pushed forward. His empty stomach was pleading with him otherwise. His legs were tired and weak but the hope that there could be some resemblance of food over this hill or the next kept him going. The wind was now thick with the odor of smoke, and the farmer could feel a new pain throbbing in his bad arm, as if his body were reacting to the memories of slaughter and despair that smell brought back. But he was no longer the soldier that could fight and kill his enemies. He was now just a poor, starving farmer with a shattered arm desperately looking for food in a ruined landscape.

From the top of the hill he could see a plume of pitch-black smoke staining the horizon, like an ugly scar torn across the grey skies. A raiding party must be close by, burning any dwelling they found. The farmer stood there on the crest of the hill momentarily, staring at the smoke. If he continued in the direction of the raiding party's path, he would be exposing himself to a danger that he wouldn't be able to fight. The thought seemed to be an unnatural contradiction of the will to survive that God gave every living thing. But if there was going to be food anywhere in this desolate and broken wilderness, it would be wherever the soldiers were travelling to.

The cottage must have collapsed in on itself when the flames enveloped and overwhelmed it. Now it was just a smoldering heap of charred wood and crackling thatch. Sparks still drifted through the wind. The chicken coop had been smashed almost to pieces, and all of its inhabitants taken leaving a trail of scattered feathers and broken eggs leading back to the road. They obviously hadn't found a way to take the single goat this family had as well, and had cut its throat. The farmer could see its chest continue to rise up and down slightly, as the blood still flowed from the gash across his throat, sticking to his white coat and mattering it. The farmer then found the goat's owners.

The younger man was laid flat out near the road, blankly staring up at the sky. He had had a spear rammed through his chest where he had stood, leaving a chasm like hole where his chest plate had been, which made his insides quite visible. The farmer leaned down and used his good hand to close his eyes. A slight walk up the road and the old man was crumpled up against a tree. A bloody mask covered his face, seeping down from a wound on his forehead. From slightly examining his body, the farmer could see that both his legs had snapped under the pressure of repeated stamps and kicks.

After repeated exposure to every hideous experience the battlefield had to offer, the sight of these two men simply washed over the farmer. It was what was hanging from the tree directly above the old man that pierced his eyes, and leaked to the back of his head where it would fester and haunt him along with all his other worst memories until he departed from this world.

The young woman was young, and beautiful. Yes, she must have been a true beauty. She was hanging at the end of the rope, slowly drifting to the side to side in the light breeze. Her skin was grey and discolored. He could not see her eye color, as they had rolled into the back of her skull. Her dress was torn, and the hem of it hanging down by her bare feet. The entire lower half of her dress was bloody, from where the farmer assumed they had raped her. As he stared up at her, he felt warm tears prick his eyes. How was it possible for God to create such a beautiful thing, and then allow it to be ripped from his world in such a savage and undignified way?

The old man suddenly let out a loud, agonized cry. The farmer's moment of grief was abruptly finished as he leapt back at the sound. The old man desperately sucked in air, and started saying incomprehensible words in a voice stifled by fear. He then let out a short shriek of agony, as the pain in his ruined legs returned to him. The farmer crouched down next to him, watching him. The old man was blinded by the bloody mask coating his face, and his hands were fumbling around on the ground as he tried to get his bearings.

There was nothing here anymore for the farmer to forage. He had to leave. But he could not just allow the old man to stay here, blind and paralysed. Would the cold eventually take him? Or maybe hunger or the pain. The farmer winced at the image of a wolf journeying down from the woods and preying on the dying man. The beast tearing away pieces of flesh as he still breathed. The farmer knew that it would not be human of him to leave this old man here to slowly die alone, but of course he also needed to move on.

He decided to do something he had not done since he had dropped his sword in terror and fled the field at Hastings, cradling his freshly broken arm as he did so. He wrapped his good hand firmly around the old man's neck, who jolted back at the touch of an unseen person. A moment of doubt stopped the farmer briefly. But after a short while, he used the available strength in his good arm and started to squeeze.

The camp fire was the sole light in the pitch black covering the moor. And the laughter and babbling of the soldiers in their strange language pierced the heavy nighttime silence. The farmer laid down watching them, trying to avoid the sentries. Following the raiding party had led him straight to them, and he knew that they had hoarded food in the camp.

He crept slowly forward, searching for a way in through the tents maybe. He stifled a cry of pain with great difficulty, as he pushed too much weight on to his bad arm. He gritted his teeth tightly together, and pushed an agonized yelp back down into his body.

He then pushed himself forward across the wet grass with more urgency towards the nearest tent. He could feel the warmth of their campfire on his face, and could hear them hungrily smacking their lips together as they ate. The farmer was now letting his hunger think for him, and not his better judgement. He had not eaten anything for nearly three days now, and the emptiness in his stomach had turned into pain. A pain which grew with each missed opportunity and chance wasted. His good arm began to work more urgently and furiously as the camp edged ever closer to him, only to abruptly stop when the hobnailed boot stamped down on the back of his head.

The farmer woke being dragged across the grass by both his arms, which were now twisted into awkward positions. His return to consciousness was greeted with a pain shooting up and down his bad arm. He could feel warm blood tricking down the back of his neck, as a burning orange blur in front of him eventually took form into the campfire.

The two soldiers threw him down on to the ground, as their comrades stood up in alarm to study him. Their faces contorted with hate. They started furiously talking to each in their language, as one of them placed a heavy kick to the farmer's ribs. Some of them laughed as the farmer curled up in pain and whimpered like a dog being disciplined. He saw a brief flash of white, as one of them drew his sword.

He was pulled up on to his knees by the same two men, as the soldier with the drawn sword approached. The other men eagerly gathered around, expecting to see more blood. The men holding him let him drop to the ground, his hands now on the floor as his executioner stood over him. He could feel the cold steel of the blade touch the back of his neck, as if his soon-to be killer were savoring the moment.

The farmer stared at the ground, and dug his hands into the soil defiantly. After all the battles he had survived and times he could have easily been killed, this was how he would die; on his knees as he searched for food. He asked them to get over with it quickly and give him some dignity, but they obviously did not understand him.

Suddenly a much taller soldier, at least a head taller than most of the others burst through the assembled audience. He wore a black cloak hanging from his shoulders and had a natural air of command. The men stopped what they were doing immediately, and the farmer could hear him barking what sounded like orders and impatient questions. Their commander stopped in front of him, and the farmer could feel him grasp his hair and painfully pull his head up.

The farmer wearily looked up at the tall dark figure, who suddenly stopped motionless, as he appeared to study the farmer's face from under his helmet. He could feel the grip of the gloved hand loosen on his hair, as the commander slowly knelt down to bring his face level with the farmer's. Time seemed to pass very slowly as this new soldier stared at him intently with pale blue eyes, the rest of his face still obscured by his helmet, which he then quickly removed. A surprisingly young face with short cropped black hair.

And then the farmer's mind threw him back to the field at Hastings three years before. The particular memory in mind was when one of the Conqueror's knights had fallen in front of the shield wall, his horse cut out from under him. The horse writhed on the ground in pain, and the knight clattered to the ground squarely in front of the farmer. The rest of the knights retreated back down the hill to their lines. The farmer stepped forward out of the shield wall, ready to administer the killing blow. As he raised his axe, he could see the youthful looks and terrified blue eyes staring up at him. The same face staring into his eyes now in this camp. The same man.

In that moment, the farmer had kept his axe raised in the air for a few seconds. He did not want to kill this young man, there was no need. This boy's army had arrived in the farmer's country to pillage and conqueror, but he was not personally responsible for that. His sword was out of reach and he could not fight back. What was the point in taking his life? The farmer lowered his axe, and gestured for the young man to rejoin his army. He had looked up at the farmer almost confused, as if he had expected to die. He remained sat on the ground in disbelief before the farmer gestured for him to leave again. This time he quickly obliged, and ran down the hill to his lines. The farmer returned to the shield wall.

Later that day the shield wall broke. The farmer's shield, along with his arm underneath had shattered under another knight's lance, the King had been killed and the whole army disintegrated, granting the invaders freedom to spread terror and death throughout the land. Yet through all that, the farmer had somehow survived. And it seemed that escaping death again was God's reward for sparing a single life on that day three years.

Morning broke over the moor. Orange beams of sunlight penetrated through the clouds, illuminating the way home for the farmer. He briskly walked from hill to hill, his strength returned. His good arm held over his shoulder a sack full of bread, meat, vegetables and even a container of ale.

Last night he had gorged himself on all the food the young commander had to offer. The young man had stayed with him, sat down next to him watching him eat, seeing if there was anything more he needed. He even offered the farmer a tent, but his guest declined. The farmer wanted to go home now. They did not understand each other's languages but they seemed to have an understanding of each other. The young soldier watched with sadness as the farmer left his camp.

After regaining his bearings in the wilderness, the farmer's cottage eventually came into view. A lonely grey shape surrounded by hills on three sides, and a stream on another. The farmer stopped abruptly when he saw it. These three days had taken their toll. He had been driven to abandon dignity and scrape for food like an animal, he had witnessed widespread death and suffering, and escaped death by a coincidence. Returning home would not feel the same again.

He approached the door, which was still hanging by its hinges just about. In his absence, animals had probably come and foraged, perhaps slept in his home overnight. He noticed that just in front of the house, grass was starting to cover his wife's grave. He had only dug that hole in the ground and laid her to rest inside before he left. Now nature was starting to reclaim that small patch of earth, like what it does with us all when we have had our time.

Instead of going inside, the farmer decided to sit down in front of his house. Next to her. He had not dug her a very deep or suitable grave, given that he had very little strength remaining at the time. He had rushed it, as he wanted to leave as quickly as possible and forage for food. He would not accept the same fate that had befallen her. The last few days had been so desperate, the farmer had yet to even start mourning her.

He eased himself down next to her, finding a comfortable position. He then carefully looked through the sack of food, and found the container of ale. He then contently sipped the ale, looking out on the moor, which now seemed quite peaceful. He could not smell that stench of death that had hung over the land any more. At least for now, things had returned to normal. The door of course needed to be repaired, as did many other parts of the cottage. And at some point, he needed to think about replacing the heard of sheep the invaders had stolen from him. But right now, the farmer just wanted to sit down next to his wife, and drink his ale.

THE CAVE

A freezing breeze whistled through the cave. It chilled Captain Jameson so that he retreated further into the tattered old coat which he had lifted from a fisherman's hut months ago. It brought with it the now all too familiar odour of sea salt which hung in the air and assaulted his nostrils.

At first the smell brought back fond memories of where he grew up on the west coast of Ireland, when him and his younger brother would race each other along the windswept beaches and up the paths ascending the cliffs. Now it made him feel almost sick. It clung to his already stinking clothes, embedded itself in his unkempt mangled hair and somehow got under his fingernails.

The smell was as constant as the ever-present crash of waves against the cliff face. A ceaseless crescendo dominating every second of his existence. There when he woke, there when he went to sleep. If he ever left this cave, he was sure it would be echoing in his head forever after.

After surveying the endless grey sea from the mouth of the cave, he retreated back into the depths of the cliff. There in the half darkness, his men were huddled around a campfire. Nine of them present. The illuminating orange glow of the fire revealing the strain, depression and hopelessness on their gaunt faces. The best soldiers in the world. Now reduced to living a miserable existence in a cave.

It had been nearly eight months now since the French landed. The Navy had sunk to the bottom of the Straits of Gibraltar, leaving the Army as England's last hope. The men of the British Army distinguished themselves in battle, as they always did. But courage wasn't enough against Napoleon's *Armee d'Anglaterre*; a vast force in the hundreds of thousands drawn from across Europe. Most formations fought to the very end. Captain Jameson's regiment had been decimated somewhere outside of Exeter, its survivors scattered in all directions across the countryside.

He had forgotten for how long they had been hiding here. One man had started to scratch a tally into the wall of the cave, counting the days spent cowering from the enemy in what was essentially a large hole in a cliff. But even he had given up, as if he realised there was no point in it. The agonisingly long days were spent hoping for the slim chance that somebody might find them, give them new orders and they would finally have a reason to leave this place. But since that day when most of Jameson's command was torn to shreds by artillery, crushed by an onslaught of lancers or slaughtered in that bayonet charge, he had not received any news from the outside world.

He had no idea if the remnants of the Army were continuing to fight elsewhere, how far the French had advanced or what had happened to the King and Parliament. All there was, was the cave.

A foraging party of three men returned, and immediately rushed to the fire to warm themselves. They had left early in the morning, and had raided a nearby farm for vegetables and poultry. The party's leader; Corporal Harris had been a professional thief before he had been forced to join the Army, and was an expert in moving without others sensing his presence and stealing from them before they realised anything was wrong.

The survival of the men in the cave depended upon the success of these excursions. Most of what the men had eaten in the last few months had been stolen, from vegetable patches, chicken coups or fishing boats in the surrounding area or from a village a few miles down the coast. They had to be quiet and leave no evidence of being there. They were unsure if there were any French patrols in the area, but couldn't afford to assume that there weren't any.

The loyalties of the local populace were also questionable. It was no secret by now that the desperately poor communities in the countryside would turn in hiding soldiers to the French, if it meant filling their bowls for a few more days. The people here therefore couldn't be trusted, as they eked out a meagre existence on this unforgiving stretch of coast. Also, most of them seemed to speak Cornish as their mother tongue and only spoke English through a thick, impenetrable accent. It was doubtful if they even considered themselves English. Jameson knew that they didn't have any friends here.

Corporal Harris and his party hadn't had the most successful of trips. All they had to show for their efforts were a few cabbages and a single rooster, which hung from Harris' belt having already had its neck rung. Before Jameson could say anything, Harris made his excuse. "The farmer over the hill rose earlier today", he grunted in his strange accent which Jameson placed to the marshes of the Thames estuary. "We could only take what we have 'ere". He didn't make eye contact with Jameson, and instead looked down at his muddy boots or made nervous glances at the other men.

Some of the men gathered around the campfire groaned or swore in disappointment, while others looked to each other helplessly as if asking for a solution. Jameson tried his best to maintain a cool unaffected exterior as any good officer should, but he knew that this was a big problem. They had all agreed together not to go out foraging more than three times in one week, otherwise they risked revealing their presence to the locals. The men would go even hungrier for the next few days.

As if spurned by a painful feeling of failure, Harris suddenly changed his tone from abject shame to an almost violent rage. "We could 'ave more food if we got rid of 'im!", he exploded, pointing angrily down into the dark interior of the cave. All the men looked in the direction he was pointing, as if confirming that he had a good point.

Down there, hidden in the darkness was Private Williams. He had been tied up, dragged into the pitch black of the deepest part of the cave and left there. Although no sound came from the darkness to confirm that Williams was even alive down there, they could all tell that he was listening.

About a week ago, Williams had been caught trying to steal an extra ration of rum while the men were sleeping. He had been beaten mercilessly by some of the men, before having both his hands and feet painfully tied behind his back and left in the dark. Jameson had disagreed vehemently with the mens' conduct. They had not conducted themselves like soldiers. But he kept his feelings to himself, because truthfully, he was now scared of his own men after the incident had occurred.

They had all agreed that that evening they would put Williams on trial, so he could speak for himself and then they could decide what to do with him. Harris and a few others had been demanding that they deal with him immediately, but Jameson had argued the case that they should listen to the man in question and rationally determine together the best course of action. They had agreed albeit reluctantly, much to Jameson's surprise. It was a display of authority from him which he realised afterwards had been increasingly rare recently. If he wasn't careful, he would lose control over them. But he started to think that that control had maybe already slipped away.

That evening, Williams was pulled from the depths of the cave and thrown down by the campfire where the men; thirteen in total were all gathered to decide his fate. Williams had never been an especially big man; he had a thin pale face, twig like arms and his uniform always hung off of his slight body. Now he looked frailer than ever, almost skeletal in his appearance. The skin on his face seemed to stretch across his skull like a mask. Ugly dark bruises wrapped themselves around his wrists from where the men had ruthlessly fastened his bounds. The constant stress and fear of his situation had caused his hair to fall out, leaving it in messy patches dotted over his scalp. Williams had an air of resignation about him. His face showed no emotion, and his eyes betrayed no light or spark and appeared almost like dark lifeless slits in his head. It was as if all the hunger, beatings and helplessness had exhausted him more than anything else. He was just now waiting for the end.

Jameson mediated the proceedings. He found himself raising his voice on several occasions in sometimes futile attempts to bring order to the trial. Harris and his group of acolytes which had flocked to him demanded repeatedly that he needed to punished for his crimes, which they claimed amounted to cowardice and treason. When some spoke up to encourage sympathy and understanding of his circumstances, they were shouted down. Through all of this, Williams lay bound on the stony floor of the cave. He never said anything, even when called upon to speak. His silence was met with more jeers and aggression by Harris and his band. "Hang him!" they repeatedly demanded.

After over an hour of seemingly endless arguing and bickering which reached no conclusion, Jameson raised his hand to plea for silence. They didn't notice him until Harris told everyone to shut up and listen to their commanding officer. A deafly silence descended over them, only the sound of the waves smashing into the rocks as usual remained.

Jameson made a speech which he been rehearsing in his head over and over again the last hour. He asked the men to remember that they were soldiers and to act accordingly. He told them to still think of Williams as one of their own. Yes, his actions were regrettable but given their own circumstances, they should be able to comprehend them. Lastly, he made the point that if they were going to be divided and turn on men they had trained, marched and fought with, then there truly was no hope of them defeating the French.

After he had finished speaking, the men looked around to each other. Some with looks of shame, others looked encouraged. Encouraged that their commanding officer had finally spoken up to reaffirm that they were still soldiers not a pack of miserable cave-dwellers, and that as long as they stuck together, they had a way out of this place.

Although the silence persisted for what felt like a very long time, a warm feeling of gratification started to creep over Jameson. His gamble had worked. But he had failed to notice Harris in this time, whose face contorted with silent fury before he eventually exploded with his usual hatred and rage. "We should 'ave expected this from a paddy!" he spat. "No one trust this paddy!" he bellowed at the top of his lungs to the men.

Harris had struck Jameson's Achilles heel. He had been raised in Ireland, but had always felt nothing but English. His father; a wealthy landowner who had fought at Quebec, had raised him to be English, and to be proud of that fact. Yet Jameson had always felt a strong connection to the country he grew up in. He even felt sympathies for the Irish peoples' struggle, which he kept to himself. All of his childhood friends had been the sons of his father's tenants, back in those early days when things like politics and nationality were not important.

Why this suddenly all mattered on this night was because of the stories that swept the Army shortly after the invasion. The Irish battalions had supposedly been overjoyed at the arrival of the French, who had come to conquer their own masters. Accounts spoke of Irish soldiers laying down their weapons and refusing to fight, sometimes even murdering their English officers. The most troubling tales for Jameson were of those men siding with the French, swapping their red coats for blue ones, and committing to killing as many Englishmen as possible. If the stories were true, Jameson didn't think about what might have happened to the English families still living in Ireland, like his parents and brother.

He didn't even dare think about that. Yet now where he grew up was being used against him, being used to question his suitability for command and even his own loyalty.

Within a few seconds, most of the men had turned on Jameson. An almost deafening crescendo of threats and accusations directed at him shattered the silence of the cave. Without realising it, Jameson had lost their obedience and trust. For whatever motivation; it could have been a hatred of officers and the authority they represented, a desire for power himself over others or simply anger at his circumstances, Harris had slithered his way into the mens' heads and poisoned their thoughts against Jameson. He had had an enemy in this cave, under his own command all this time without realising it.

Harris eventually beckoned for silence. A simple raise of the hand was enough for them to withhold their rage, at least for the time being until he wanted to use it for his own devious reasons again. Jameson was stunned into a desperate silence himself, looking at the hateful faces of men he thought he had known so well before. He was not their commander anymore, and he had been oblivious to it.

Harris looked like he was deeply satisfied with his position of power, and taking great pleasure in Jameson's displacement and humiliation. A twisted grin spread across his pockmarked face, revealing his crooked decaying teeth. "How do you plead to the charges, Captain?".

Williams stumbled down on the path in front of Jameson. He had needed to be dragged out of the cave after the sentence had been passed, and forced to his feet. He had problems standing, as there simply wasn't enough strength left in his legs to support him after the days of starvation. Also, he was finally showing signs of collapsing under the fear and despair of what was coming next.

"On your feet!" growled Private Morgan, standing over his prisoner, bearing his musket tightly in his big hands. He first savagely kicked Williams in his side, who gave a shrill cry as the air was forced out of him. He was then once more pulled aggressively to his feet. William's face was creased with grief and desperation, and let out a few agonised sobs. Tears were now running profusely down his bony cheeks. They continued on towards the cliffs.

The trial had concluded with an overwhelming vote for both Jameson and Williams to be sentenced to hang for their treason. When they realised that they did not have a sufficient amount of rope or an accessible place to hang the pair of them, they opted to have them thrown from the high cliffs overlooking the cave instead.

Harris had ordered Private Morgan, as the strongest man in the group to escort the traitors to the cliff and carry out the sentence. It was an order which Morgan did not seem too pleased with, but had to comply with or risk facing his new commander's judgement himself. They reached the highest peak of the cliffs as dawn was breaking, the pitch-black night sky had been swept away by a pale blue canvas reaching towards the horizon. Below them, the sea stretched off into the distance, it was remarkably calm in the early morning breeze.

Upon seeing the precipice where the cliffs began, Williams collapsed to the ground again in sheer terror, and lay on his side. He started sucking in huge gasps of air in an ineffective attempt to compose himself. He reminded Jameson of a fish torn from the sea, flailing and struggling on the deck of a boat. Jameson just simply stood rooted to the spot he was standing, and hung his head down, looking at the ropes tightly binding his hands. There was nothing he could do now.

He had survived several campaigns in India and somehow made it through the invasion, when most of his close friends and colleagues had been unceremoniously killed in various ways on the battlefield. Now he was going to end being hurled from this cliff by one of his men. Morgan; the man in question was pacing up and down the lip of the cliff, searching for the best place to carry out his orders with grim workmanship. Suddenly he stopped and knelt down on the grass, closely examining a potential spot. He then stood up slowly and let out a mournful sigh.

Morgan then slung his musket over his back, before turning around and striding back with renewed vigour to where Williams was still lying on the ground. He wrapped his big muscular arms around William's feeble body and hauled him to the ground. Instantaneously, Williams started crying and pleading. Pleading to Morgan, to God, to anyone. With great ease Morgan pulled him towards the edge, and in a split second Williams was plummeting down the slide of the cliff-face.

There was a scream, which sounded more like a wail which continued for an excruciating few seconds before it abruptly stopped. Morgan's had worn a look of anguish on his round bearded face through the whole ordeal, and although it had only lasted seconds, looked drained by it. As Williams plummeted to the rocks below, Jameson had felt a warm stream of urine flow down his right leg. In those seconds, a flurry of different feelings swelled in him.

First there was a sinking sensation, as if something had

just hit the bottom of his stomach. The realisation that this really was the end of him. Then as the heat of his own urine stung against the side of his leg, a sudden fury boiled up inside him.

Morgan surveyed the scene down below, searching for Williams' body. He still had his musket slung over his back. He had precariously positioned himself by the edge. Jameson's hands were tightly bound but he needed to do something now. He had to fight. Morgan started to turn his big body around towards his second prisoner. Jameson lowered his head, and charged.

As soon as the innkeeper placed the bread and cheese in front of Jameson, he devoured it with great relish. He chomped down on his meal, greedily smacked his lips together and paid no attention to the crumbs he was scattering over his host's table. There was no time to gracefully conduct himself with the etiquette expected of an officer. The events of the previous night and on the cliff had left him in a daze, his mind completely exhausted by the never-ending cycle of fear, despair and helplessness that had consumed him.

The innkeeper; a large, round faced man wearing an apron, then tentatively gave him a large clay mug of water. He looked at Jameson with a mixture of great curiosity and concern, as his guest poured the contents of the mug down his throat, making almost animalistic slurping sounds and spilling a great deal of it down his chin and front.

Jameson had wandered the nearby fields and lanes aimlessly, his hands still bound together looking for any semblance of food or shelter. After what had felt like a long while, he turned a corner around a high stonewall at the edge of a farm, only to find himself directly in the path of a young girl.

She had curly red hair and freckled round face, and was carrying a large pale of water that looked nearly as big as her. The two of them stopped and stared at each other for a few seconds, both of them unsure of what to say or do next. Jameson realised with a sharp pang of dread how he must look to this little girl; his tattered uniform, filthy face and hair, his hands still bound. But instead of dropping her pale of water and running in terror away from him, to his surprise she calmly beckoned to him to come and follow her. "I live nearby" she said in a low quiet voice.

When he reached the small fishing village where the girl lived, he found that his fears about the locals had been proved wrong. The innkeeper; the girl's father had hurried him inside, and cut the rope binding his hands with a bread knife. The feeling of blood returning to his numb pale hands was a sensation which warmed his whole body.

After a short while, the innkeeper sat down next to Jameson to ask him several carefully worded questions about who he was and where he was from. Jameson told him about what had happened to his regiment in the invasion, about his men and the cave, but didn't mention the trial or Williams or what had happened at the cliff. The memory of it was still too raw to tell anyone.

Yet Jameson did not ask the innkeeper about news of the invasion and the broader picture of events. He was not interested in that right now. As she was recuperating at his hospitable host's dinner table, he started brooding on those events. He had been stripped of his command, humiliated, condemned to death by men he thought he could trust. The initial relief and joy of having escaped the cliff was starting to be replaced by something else.

A hatred had started to smoulder at the back of his mind, as he sat there, eating a second helping of bread. He began to revisit the memory of those events, and felt a shiver of the terror he experienced reverberate down his spine. That terror provided the fuel to the now blazing fire consuming his thoughts. The anger making him curl his hands into tight fists, his dirty jagged fingernails scrapping against the surface of the table as he did so.

He wanted them to pay. To suffer. Especially Harris. His ugly wicked smile was now an image which kept on resurfacing in Jameson's mind, making him feel sick to his stomach. He couldn't wait to see what expression Harris would have on his face after he realised that the tables had turned, that Jameson now had him at his mercy.

He had one thought on his mind now. And things like loyalty and country no longer counted. He turned to the innkeeper and asked; "Where is the nearest French garrison?"

Index

M3 Lee and Other Stories

Finito di stampare nel mese di novembre 2020
presso Rotomail Italia S.p.A. - Vignate (MI)